# Grandmother Wolf

## and Other Stories

I0452411

*Cover Art © Peter Mates*

*Grandmother Wolf and Other Stories*

*FootSteps Press First Edition*
*Typeset by Daniel Nanavati*

*ISBN 978-1-908867-41-4*

# Grandmother Wolf

## and Other Stories

## Frances Oliver

Frances Oliver has published six novels and a book of short stories, and self-published three memoirs. She was born in Vienna, grew up in the USA, and has since lived, worked and travelled in a number of countries, finally settling in Cornwall. When not writing she devotes much time to environmental campaigns.

By the same author:

*All Souls,*
*The Tourist Season*
*Xargos*
*Children of Epiphany*
*The Peacock's Eye*
*Dancing on Air (stories)*
*The Ghosts of Summer*

Memoirs:
*Girl in a Freudian Slip*
*Jaundiced in Antalya*
*Farewell to William Tell*

# PREFACE & SOURCES

In the introduction I wrote to my first collection of more or less ghostly stories, 'Dancing on Air', Ash-Tree Press, 2004, I said that not all were proper ghost stories but all involved hauntings of one kind or another.

Obsessions are hauntings, as are certain memories or fears... The stories in this book, however, are definitely in the occult realm, except for one little dystopic tale, 'Dispension Island'. In the age of climate crisis, I find it impossible not to include something post-apocalyptic, though the time for warnings is long past.

Three of the stories, inspired by a raised tombstone, a house name, and a poem have their own little introductions. 'Peripheral Vision' was inspired by a *trompe l'oeil* painting. In a way it is a sequel to the title story of my first collection. As that story has been published twice, once in my Ash-Tree Press book and again in the 'Best American Horror' collection for that year, I didn't want to use it again; but any reader who is puzzled by what the ouija board says in 'Peripheral Vision' could turn to the 'Dancing on Air' story to find out. Both 'Dancing on Air' and 'Peripheral Vision' were written years before the Covid pandemic.

I have included one story from the previous collection, 'Prester John'. I cannot resist seeing in print again the wonderful flamboyant medieval texts that led to this story. If we find those myths bizarre, think of the bizarre myths of unrestricted free-market capitalism and mandatory economic growth that are destroying the world.

'Prester Joh'n and 'The Afterthought', depicting a centuries-old children's game, were both inspired by old books found in the Morrab Library, Penzance. Long may their old books live.

'The Saracen Girl' was first conceived as a story, metamorphosed into the beginning of my last novel, 'Taking the Waters', and is here back as a story again. Other writers have done this, notably – in reverse – the brilliant (if now so politically incorrect) Evelyn Waugh, whose story 'The Man Who Loved Dickens' became the somewhat incongruous end to his novel 'A Handful of Dust'.

'The King of Majorca', inspired by a real statue, was first printed in the anthology 'Shades of Darkness', Ash-Tree Press, 2008.

All the other stories are new to this collection.

I shun 'Acknowledgements' but I do want to say thank you to Daniel Nanavati and once again, Jennifer Hart

For
Josie Aigner
and
Rebecca Verschaeve

# Stories

# The King of Majorca

Annemarie Bernfeld, the child of European refugee parents now living in New York (*wrote Marianne Laubfeld, the child of European refugee parents now living in New York*) was sent to spend her junior year abroad in the war-scarred France of 1951 (*wrote Marianne Laubfeld, a college freshman, taking a two month summer course on French civilization in the town of Perpignan in the war-scarred France of 1951*).

Annemarie was a quiet studious girl with no intimate friends, who seemed timid and almost startled when spoken to. Her apparent detachment from everything except her studies was a great worry to her parents, who spent vast amounts of money on her education and on therapy to 'normalise' this dreamy, withdrawn child, already diagnosed by the more mercenary of the therapists as borderline schizophrenic. It was hoped by everyone concerned with Annemarie that the excitement of a new culture and a new country would wake this frail sleeping beauty from her mysterious dreams.

These hopes were vain. The shuttered houses, the lazy afternoons, the somehow somnolent sunlight of Pontrieux (*why doesn't she use the real name of the place, thought the young tutor, irritably, and circled 'somehow somnolent sunlight' and wrote in the margin, 'avoid overdoing alliteration'*), lost in its own dusty dreams under the icy indifferent glare of the distant Pyrenees, did nothing to rouse Annemarie from her solitary reveries. She moved through Pontrieux like someone behind a wall of glass, a pale, pretty girl with an absent smile, seeming not to hear either the old women in black who muttered about her young American wealth or the tanned louts in white who longed for her young American body. But of course she did hear them, and her sensitive soul recoiled from the avoidances of one, and the advances of the other. Secretly, she gave all her allowance to the beggars who haunted the streets, and wore her oldest clothes and an old scarf over her beautiful chestnut hair so that the idle ogling young men in the cafés would leave her alone.

Annemarie's fellow students, apparently staggering from the shock of a different culture, and full of nostalgia for popcorn and Coke, indulging themselves in endless gossip about who had, might have, or seemed about to sleep with whom, left her as indifferent as were the shining peaks on the heat-blurred horizon. Even the attentions of Mark Cromley, a boy brighter and more perceptive than the others, were not welcome.

"You want a knight in shining armour," Annemarie's practical earthy mother had been fond of telling her, with derision. Like all conventional mothers she hoped that Annemarie's college career would bring her not so much academic success and a truly broadened mind as the chance to meet, marry and be a fit wife for a good solid professional man. Annemarie had laughed her rare musical laugh and said "If I ever find the knight, Mother, I won't even mind if the armour is not shiny. I will polish it myself."

The strange truth is that Annemarie's unimaginative mother was actually close to the mark. Annemarie was in love, deeply, unhealthily perhaps, in love with the Middle Ages. Perhaps it was part of that syndrome which makes small children fixate on dinosaurs, the dawn of the world's history corresponding to the dawn of their own; adolescent Annemarie's absorption in what historians call the adolescent period of European civilization. (*Good thought,' wrote the tutor, then finding that fatuous, crossed out 'good' and wrote 'interesting' instead.*) Something in Annemarie called to ruined towers and soaring arches and the gem-like brilliance of stained glass, to Arthurian legend and Gregorian chant, as something in other girls called to Van Johnson and Cary Grant. Perhaps her father's small collection of Gothic artifacts had imprinted her childhood mind; perhaps there was some truth in the Tarot-inspired speculations of Lucy Dawes, her one close friend, who said that Annemarie was the reincarnation of a young chatelaine who had been burned as a Cathar heretic at Montségur, and that what drew her to the Middle Ages was that unfinished, brutally severed life.

Lucy herself had died of polio at only sixteen, and this was a major reason for Annemarie's present solitude. Lucy's death had thrown her back yet more into her obsession, yet more upon herself. So Pontrieux was both the best and the worst place for Annemarie, a town of ancient glories where the past was more real than the drab, impoverished present. And in fact had not the horrors of the war years been medieval, and those who fought the ultimate horror of Nazism like the deluded knights of the Crusades – only not deluded and therefore more shining than those armoured warriors themselves?

One would think this last thought might have made Annemarie turn to the present, that some hero of the Resistance might have satisfied her fantasies. But Annemarie was incapable of contact with real flesh and blood. A premature and traumatic sexual experience, whose awfulness we mercifully need not dwell upon here (*Robert North, the young tutor, did dwell on it a minute, wondering what the awful experience might have been*), had made her incapable of physical response to the opposite sex, and except for her romantic friendship with Lucy, in which whatever sexual element there may have been was entirely latent, she was not attracted either by her own.

So Annemarie went through the motions, did her assignments in Medieval Studies and Provençal French – her dream was to devote herself entirely to studies in that language, to make research on the troubadour poets and especially the Cathar ones her life's work – not only adequately but well, and spent her spare time wandering the cobbled Pontrieux streets or sitting in neglected cafés sipping bitter coffee and staring at fifteenth century ramparts, with the words of some old ballad singing in her head.

For some reason, however, though it was the building that should have attracted her most, she avoided entering the cathedral. She told herself that it was because the cathedral was the *pièce de résistance*, that she wanted to see everything else first and not be distracted from her college work. But the truth was something different. Whenever she approached the cathedral, a strange feeling seized her, a mix of apprehension and expectation, of joy and fear, as though some marvellous assignation awaited her, but also danger. It was the fear that won out. She would say to herself, 'This is ridiculous', and then her steps would drag, and it was as if something stronger and wiser than herself pulled her back. She would think, trying to ignore how odd this all was, trying to make some excuse to herself for her erratic behaviour, "It's too late today, I need more time, I'll go tomorrow." Then tomorrow again she would not go.

At last there came a day when, pursued by a particularly persistent local boy (*that alliteration again, thought Robert, but did not mark it*), who was actually threatening to make a pass at her on the street, Annemarie fled into the cathedral literally as a refuge, as so many in the Middle Ages did – her fear now of the importunate stranger being greater than that mystifying apprehension which always seized her at the cathedral's door.

At first she was afraid the stranger might follow, or wait for her outside. Then, as she heard his loud exclamation of '*Merde, alors*' and his retreating steps, she felt more at ease, and began to examine the turgid gloaming in which she found herself.

But she spent little time admiring the soaring Gothic arches, the curious fonts, the exquisitely carved reredos. She ignored the famous crucifix with its agonised face, skeletal body, and gaping wooden wounds. She was drawn almost at once to a marble crusader tomb lit with flickering tapers, a figure with hands clasped on a sword-hilt and a lion at its feet. No, not a crusader, but a king, his crowned head resting on a tapestried and tasselled marble pillow, his robes reaching down to the lion's sleeping form.

The statue's marble eyes were closed as was fitting, but the mouth was faintly curled in a strange half-smile. It was a face at once ascetic and sensual, marked by who knew what triumph or failure, passion or pain, the face of someone who carried a rare but bitter wisdom into his tomb. To Annemarie the face was more beautiful than a Botticelli angel, or even Rembrandt's 'Man with the Golden Helmet' who seems imbued with that same wisdom, that same bitterness. Yet for all its transcendent, almost Buddha-like quality the colourless marble of the face seemed to have the plasticity, the warmth of human flesh. If she gazed at that face long enough, thought Annemarie, might not some profound and powerful secret be revealed to her, something that would change her life forever and bring peace to a soul bewildered and stunned by the cruelty and blindness of the world?

When at last she tore herself away and reached the waning sunlight outside, she realised with a shock that she had been gazing at the mysterious marble effigy for almost an hour, though it seemed to her only minutes had gone by. On her way out of the churchyard she passed a bent old priest hurrying to evensong. Timidly she stopped him and asked if he knew anything about the royal tomb in the transept. The priest told her it was the tomb of the King of Majorca who had laid the cathedral's foundation stone. No, there were no legends, nothing that he knew. And now, he added, annoyed by this gormless American with her faltering questions about matters of no consequence, he must hurry to his religious duties.

From then on Annemarie haunted the cathedral. Every spare minute was now spent in its gloomy precincts. Often, too, she stayed through services, perched quietly in a pew mumbling and crossing herself, kneeling and rising with the rest, stealing a glance whenever she dared at the silent knight in the transept. When they were alone together she gazed at the King's face until her legs were cramped and aching, her body stiff, her eyes swimming and the blood singing in her ears. Now the fear and joy, the expectation and apprehension, were still there, but the desire that filled her with these contradictory emotions was the desire to touch the King – a desire that like her initial desire to enter the cathedral steadily increased, but not without the warning fear mounting as well. And sometimes it seemed to Annemarie that the King's face changed as she watched it, that the smile grew more or less ironic or sensual or wise or remote, and sometimes it seemed to her that the eyes must open and the lips part and breathe, that the King on the tomb might suddenly spring to life.

Her studies were neglected, her classwork forgotten. She made a tentative effort to learn more about the King who obsessed her, but then decided that all she wanted to know was in the face itself – and who was to say if it was merely the sculptor's vision, not the model's, that had left it there. It was the statue that enthralled her, not the historical King. More and more in the grip of her obsession, Annemarie lost track of time; and only when a worried phone call came from her parents was she jolted into awareness that her stay in France was almost over and she must be making preparations to travel home.

The thought of being parted from the statue was almost unbearable to her, but as the date approached she knew she had neither the funds nor the excuse to stay longer. Her behaviour had become so strange that the old women who went to Mass gave her whispered curses and evil glances, and the priest himself had told her that if she came to pray she was welcome but if she came only to stare at a tomb she would do better to stay outside. In despair Annemarie decided that before she left she must contrive to spend a night in the cathedral, that if she had a whole night alone with the King of Majorca she might learn his secret, she might reach that gnosis promised in his smile.

Having decided on this desperate course, she went about it with eminent practicality. She provided herself with a flashlight, a sandwich, a thermos of hot tea; she took a warm sweater and wore sneakers so that there would be no echoing footsteps to reveal her movements. She also took a knife, not quite certain why, but thinking that knives are always useful, and that if some other intruder, some vagrant, lurked around the cathedral it might be good to have a method of defence.

After evensong, Annemarie managed to hide behind a column. She waited there, her heart pounding, her knees trembling, till the heavy door of ancient oak swung shut behind the priest, and the huge iron key turned in the lock with a grating finality that sent waves of fear coursing through her chest.

Annemarie had never seen who lit the candles

surrounding her sacred statue, or when, but there were always candles burning. Only now, as her eyes tried desperately to adjust to a darkness that seemed fluid as water and opaque as blood, she noticed that the lights were dimming, the candles flickering more and more, waning, going out. At last the only ones still burning were two candles by the statue's head. Annemarie tried her flashlight; it did not work, the battery had gone dead.

Acutely nervous now, she felt for the knife in her pocket. The she stumbled dizzily through the burgeoning darkness towards the tomb. Now there was only a weak patch of light in which she and the King of Majorca were totally alone, in total silence and total peace. Her waves of fear receded. The face, still impassive but more beautiful and mysterious than even she had ever thought it, lay naked to the fevered penetration of her gaze. As if in a trance she blew out the last candles. Then she put a hand over the marble hands on the sword hilt and bent down and put her mouth on the marble mouth.

In the morning the old sacristan, opening the cathedral doors, sensed at once that something was wrong.

Strewn in the nave were a sweater, a scarf, a flashlight, a thermos, an uneaten sandwich. The bewildered sacristan followed this trail to the tomb of the King of Majorca and then stopped dead, frozen with horror at what he saw. Prone across the statue's body lay the body of a girl, bloodstained and motionless. And the statue... Regaining his muscles and his voice, the sacristan ran screaming out of the church.

It was not until he was reinforced by priests, ambulance men, and policemen that he dared to come back. They rushed into the transept and stopped, paralysed by the same horror that had overcome the sacristan. Then one of the policemen moved to lift the girl. She was dead, cold and white as marble; the wrists she had slashed with her little knife hung limp and bloodstained at her sides. Her eyes were closed, and on her face was a mysterious half-smile, a smile of infinite experience and bitter wisdom, a smile like that on the statue's face. The statue's face, however, was no longer beautiful or pure. For the porous marble had in some bizarre fashion soaked up almost every drop of the girl's blood, so that the statue glowed like neon, no longer white but a lurid demon's red.

❈   ❈   ❈

"Miss Laubfeld," said Robert North, holding out his hand, as they were, after all, in Europe. Miss Laubfeld took it without hesitation; for one who seemed so abstracted and unsociable her handshake was surprisingly firm.

They both sat down, and there was an uncomfortable silence. Robert, not certain how to begin this tutorial, fixed his eyes on the pages before him. They had been handed in only last night, late as all the girl's course work had been. Then he began to read, "'Annemarie Bernfeld, the child of European refugee parents now living in New York –'"

"Do you have to read it out loud?"

Her voice, like her handshake, was steady, but her gaze was absent. Other people had remarked on this. *She never meets your eyes.* Her own eyes, wide and grey, were beautiful.

"I needn't go on if you don't want me to. There were just some things I wanted to point out. I've made notes in the margins. I read the beginning because – this is very autobiographical, isn't it?"

The girl answered without smiling, "That's how young people usually write. That or pure fantasy. They don't have the experience to write much else."

"So you have combined both," said Robert, and did smile. There was no smile returned. "It's a striking piece, although the statue as a sort of demon lover has, I believe, been done often before."

"It's hardly about demon love."

"I see. I think it might be read that way, though." He tried to make his voice both congenial and authoritative, and failed on both counts. "Anyhow, first of all, Miss Laubfeld – or may I say Marianne…?"

"I'll say Robert then."

This quick but flat-voiced response threw him. He found himself stammering for a moment; it happened rarely and only in moments of stress, a return to the stammer of the too pretty, too aesthetic, bullied boarding-school child. "Y-y-you were supposed to write an essay. This is an occult horror story." A genre of which he in fact heartily disapproved and one which often cropped up in composition courses, as students wrongly suppose it is the easiest thing to do.

"That assignment was like asking us to go back to school, like what did I do on my summer vacation. It wouldn't have worked for what I wanted to say."

"Okay, then. If you just tried to put that something into a non-narrative form – surely that's possible – into some kind of disquisition" – the word made her briefly and fleetingly smile – "that would have answered." He waited a moment. There was no further response.

"Try and tell me, then. At least give me an idea. What was that something you wanted to say?"

For the first time she seemed flustered. "I couldn't really say it. It kept getting away from me. So I finished with all that stuff about the girl cutting her wrists and the marble soaking up the blood, when all I wanted was to show what is in that statue's face."

"And what is in the statue's face?" Silence. "Come on, you must have at least a word or two, you're very articulate…" He was becoming impatient.

"I – listen, have you read Simone Weil?"

"A question isn't an answer," he countered gently, trying to hide that he had not, and was not even certain what Simone Weil had written.

Marianne sighed. "It's that – I only meant – okay, what's in the statue's face…" She hesitated, then spoke very quickly. "A knowledge after which nothing is possible except death."

"Well," said Robert; and said it again, "Well." He was now feeling extremely uncomfortable. He wanted to avoid the girl's gaze, then realised there was in fact no danger of meeting it: she never looked at him. She was fiddling with her pen and gazing steadily at the window as if he were not there. He found himself looking at her legs in the habitual Bermuda shorts; these legs were long, straight, muscular, and attractive, although very white. She obviously never sunbathed. Did she spend all her time in museums and churches, this girl? He steered himself back to the topic at hand. "Yes, I suppose that would be difficult to put into an essay. Still, there must be something else that has impressed you here. Could you please make another effort, and give me an essay? The continuation of this programme depends on the work we can display at the end. How about something that deals with the contrast between France and our own country? You're one of our brightest students, Marianne. I'm sure you can come up with something more relevant than this."

In the fortnight that followed, Robert North, in spite of himself, thought a great deal about Marianne Laubfeld, although he saw little of her. Sometimes she attended seminars, in which she never volunteered a word. Sometimes she was conspicuously absent; the seminars were small and her absence was more noticeable than her presence. When she was present Robert would address her with a question or two, trying, so he told himself, to draw her in, to draw her out. What he did not tell himself was that asking her questions gave him an excuse to study her face, to note again her grey eyes, her pale brown, long straight hair, the fact that her features were perfectly regular, and yet she did not *seem* beautiful — no make-up, which dimmed her in relation to the other girls, no colour, no animation, that surprising whiteness — as if she did indeed devote her hours to a candlelit cathedral. He wondered again, since the story she had given him was clearly so autobiographical, what was 'the premature and traumatic sexual experience' that had made her 'incapable of physical response to the opposite sex'. He had zealously avoided entanglement with the summer students, though more than one girl had indicated willingness to sleep with him, and Marianne at seventeen was one of the youngest, still even what was called *jail bait*, still even legally under age. He also wondered sometimes if that trauma, and her obsession with the statue, could be erased by a sexual experience of a different sort… and then, 'the knight in shining armour', he would mock himself. What a stupid and dangerous idea; and after he found his stammer returning when he spoke to Marianne, and another student giggled, he decided to address no more questions to the silent girl with the grey eyes.

The resolution was in vain. No sooner had he made it than the acting head of the summer programme called him in for a confidential consultation. "Robert, we're worried about one of the students, Marianne Laubfeld. She's started skipping her seminars, and we hear from the others that she doesn't socialize, in fact she hardly seems to be around at all. A real weirdo, the others say. No one knows where or how she passes her time, even her roommate doesn't. She just seems to disappear. I've asked your colleague Emily to talk to her and Emily's got nowhere. You're the tutor who is tackling the troubadour poets, and the course Marianne likes best, in fact the only one she now shows up for at all. Something is obviously troubling the girl; would you see if you can find what it is? Frankly, if it weren't already so late in the programme, I'd be inclined to call her parents and suggest it might be better for her to go home. She's obviously not going to get any credits for this summer."

Robert remembered another phrase from Marianne's story – curious how much of that unhealthy fantasy remained in his mind – *this dreamy withdrawn child, already diagnosed... as borderline schizophrenic.* He decided not to mention the story. "I'll t-try," he said, "but she's very difficult to approach. I don't want to make a point of it, I think that would freeze her up. Maybe tomorrow when she hands in her next assignment..." *If,* he thought, *she hands it in. If she appears at all.*

But Marianne did, and held another sheaf of papers, and even smiled at him. "I have tried," she said softly. "You said it sounded too autobiographical. Well, this one isn't like the first."

She's even wearing perfume, Robert thought as she passed him the papers; then surreptitiously he took another sniff and realized that what clung to the girl was not perfume but incense. *This one,* she said, he thought with a sinking heart.

"Read it right now if you want. It's quite short. I'd really like to know what you think of it."

*Good,* thought Robert, *this gives us a chance to talk.* "Yes, I'd like to do that," he answered quickly.

"Good," she echoed the word in his mind and sat down opposite him, holding a notebook and pen, and crossed her elegant ankles. The rest of the legs were not visible; today she was wearing a long New Look skirt. Come to think of it, every time he'd had glimpse of her lately it was a skirt she'd been wearing. Did that go with the incense? Was she spending still more time in churches and crypts and... that quiet half-smile on her face, the sudden odd amiability... what she mocking him?

Nervously, Robert began to read.

❋     ❋     ❋

*In Another Culture*

The sacristan sighed. Oh, how they bored him, these American tourists, busloads of them with their brainless chatter, their eternally clicking cameras, their naïve exclamations at anything older than fifty years.

The lot he had to deal with this afternoon was especially obnoxious. College students, come to spend a year abroad at the local university. As if there were not already Americans enough! They had plenty of time in their year to investigate his beautiful cathedral on their own – were they not godless some of them might even have chosen to attend a service or two. But no. They had to be shepherded, they had to come in a group, in a bus – young and overfed though they were, incapable of walking even from the university to the cathedral. Or perhaps they were so undisciplined and vulgar that a walking tour of the town would immediately have lost half its members to the bistros.

Now – oh misery! – this motley crew of gum-chewing barbarians was loose in his beloved cathedral, fingering the rood screen, leaning against columns, sprawling in the pews, as the professor in charge of them droned on in his execrable American French. The sacristan hurried to remonstrate with two girls whose shirts were totally sleeveless. They looked with distaste at the shawls he brought them to cover their bare arms. The sacristan insisted. "I won't wear this smelly thing. I bet it's full of germs," one of the girls said, cracking her gum. "*Je ne veux pas porter cette dirty chose,*" she added in slow spaced words of French, as if he were a small child who might not understand – and with her accent it was a wonder anyone did.

"*Alors, vous pouvez pas rester. Alors, il faut qu-quitter la cathédrale,*" rejoined the sacristan, anger making his old voice stammer and creak, and doing a rough translation in his turn, "Then you go, you no stay."

"Aw, leave us in peace, you old crow," the girl muttered half under her breath, but she kept the shawl – dropping it from her shoulders, however, the moment the sacristan's back was turned.

The professor, having switched to English, was raising his voice. "And now we come to the tomb of the King of Majorca, a truly beautiful example of a royal tomb. I would like to read to you what one of my favourite writers, Alphonse Dumoulin-Bossu, wrote about this statue. Listen carefully. Tomorrow in class I will ask you to translate this same passage into English." (Loud groans from the assembled students.) And he droned on, his pronunciation making the poor old sacristan wince.

"*Dans ce visage, ce visage un peu bizarre avec son air de misommeil et son mi sourire, c'est comme si toutes les grandes passions humaines, toute, la sensualité et l'asceticisme du moyen age, été sentiont et puis surmontés pour tomber dans une paix profonde, pour s'élever á une sagesse amère et surhumaine...*" What drivel, thought the sacristan.

Sensuality and asceticism, superhuman wisdom: why, it was almost sacrilegious – and who was this author, it did not even seem proper French.

(A neat way of excusing her grammatical errors, *thought Robert at this, and had to smile, in spite of his distress at being presented with yet another story, let alone a mere variation on the first.*) And what was he on about now in his ridiculous quotation – the candles always burning that no one had ever seen being lit? Come to think of it, who did always light those candles? Certainly not he. Some of the poor old women who haunted the cathedral, faceless shadows who crouched and mumbled in the more remote pews. But it was strange they should spend so much on candles. The poor box did not reflect such generosity, and they were more in the category of recipients than givers. Mother Jacqueline, for one. And how was it he had never once seen them placing a candle by the King?

But what was happening now? The professor was being rudely interrupted. A grinning boy with fuzzy hair standing up in cropped tufts on his head and a sweater with a big yellow letter on it was raising his hand as if he were in class, then blundering on with no invitation to speak.

"Please, Mr Mayberry – I found this funny old book in a bookshop yesterday. It's about superstitions in the Pyrenees. Listen to what it says: *'Il y a une legende que certaines statues funeraires, si on les embrasse, deviendront vivantes comme la Belle au Bois Dormant.'"* This produced a flood of giggles and, from those whose French was least advanced, cries of "Hey, translate that, Joey. What does it mean?"

"Sacrilege," muttered the sacristan, shocked, and was about to remonstrate in his quavering voice when, to his relief, the professor stopped the clamour with tones the sacristan could not mistake even if the words eluded him. "I really thinks that's rather absurd, Joe. I don't know what sort of book it is you found, but I've travelled often in the Pyrenees and have never come across any story of funerary statues wakened with a kiss like the Sleeping Beauty. Now, may we proceed?"

Soon after this the mob was ushered out. Two of the boys paused to chat in the doorway near the sacristan, who was pointedly rattling his collection box as the students passed. One was the boy Joey.

"Did you make that up, Joey?" the other boy was asking him.

"Yah," Joey whispered loudly back. "It was to tease Mary Jane. She still won't give me a date. She's such a freak about stories like that and about all the knights and armour stuff that I bet you she'll stay behind and try to wake the old marble guy with a kiss. You watch." Grinning together, they walked out. The sacristan had not really listened; he was intent on his collection box. When the last student had passed him, he noticed with a start that someone was still in the transept with the King of Majorca, a pretty girl who had looked at him with sympathy when he was insisting that other girls cover their scandalous naked arms.

"*Mam'selle*" he called out to her. "*Vos copains sont déjá partis.*"

She seemed not to hear him. He went closer and saw that her eyes were fixed on the statue's face and that she was as lost and absorbed as someone in a trance. He touched her shoulder and she jumped, like one waking from a dream. He repeated what he had said, this time in broken English. "Your friend, all going."

"*Oh, ça fait rien.*" It didn't matter. They would only go off to drink somewhere. She could do what she liked now. "*C'est permis de rester un peu içi?*"

Very well, yes, she could stay a few minutes, but only a few minutes, because he would soon be closing the cathedral to visitors, except those coming for evensong. Of course, if she wished to sit down and attend the service... she nodded absently, thanked him, and did settle herself in a pew. The sacristan soon forgot the girl and went on about his duties.

The next morning, as the sacristan neared the cathedral, his face took on an expression of bewilderment and fear.

The great door, which he remembered very well having locked, was open and swaying on its hinges. The lock was broken.

At first nothing else seemed wrong. Then he approached the tomb of the King of Majorca, and what he saw there stopped his poor old heart. The statue was gone. The marble slab held no trace of the effigy that had once lain on it, nor of the small curly-maned lion at its feet. Lying there instead was the American girl who had asked to stay behind yesterday, dead as a doornail and white as marble, her hands folded decently as if in prayer, her sneakered feet neatly crossed, and a mysterious half-smile on her little cold face.

After rapid consultation with high religious dignitaries, including even the Pope himself, it was decided this bizarre event must be hushed up as completely as possible. The press was told that the statue had been smashed and stolen and a young student from America found dead of heart failure in the church, possibly because, staying on late for private prayer, she had surprised the thieves. How the thieves had managed to break into the building, and done their dastardly work without a sound to alert anyone, were two of the puzzling aspects of the incident which were never explained.

No piece of the broken statue – it could hardly have been removed without being broken first – was ever seen again. But for some time after its disappearance, sheep and goats in the Pontrieux district were found killed and half-devoured by a mysterious wildcat, which farmers hunted in vain. After a while the livestock losses stopped and gossip about the vanished statue died down. The poor old sacristan recovered from his heart attack, but ended his days in an asylum – well cared for, at least, and reasonably peaceful, mumbling his rosary on a bench in the sun. And the boy Joey who, for a reason only his best friends suspected, suddenly lost his fun-loving frivolous habits, had his cropped hair shaved altogether, and became a monk, the only American among the Franciscan brothers in a monastery near Pontrieux.

❈    ❈    ❈

"You see," said Marianne, "why I wanted you to read it now. I want to know if it's acceptable. Emily Whatsit told me it's my last chance for a credit."

"It's another occult horror story." Robert put down his marking pencil with a gesture of exasperation.

"But it shows – what did you say? – cultural conflict. The old sacristan and the young Americans. Wasn't that the topic?"

"You were asked to write an essay."

"I don't see why the form matters so much. Anyway…" She paused. Robert waited. "Anyway, credit or not, I can't write anything else. I mean, that's all I can write. The statue – that statue – is the only thing I can write about."

This was the moment to probe, as he had been requested to do. This was the opportunity he must not lose. He began to stammer again. "A-a-a and doesn't that imply that you are obsessed with this statue? Like the girl in the story."

Marianne shrugged. Robert blundered on. "Ha-has it occurred to you that this obsession might be unhealthy? Might there be something else in your life which – which the statue symbolizes – or g-gives an escape from – whatever it is – is there something you might need to talk to someone about?" Oh God, he was so bad at this. Why did the administration ask him, of all people – and with this girl, of all people – but having started he had to continue. "You are a very intelligent girl – you are asked twice for essays, which you are perfectly capable of writing – your application for this course made that abundantly clear – and each time you hand in a horror story, and tell me you cannot write about anything except the tomb in the cathedral. Is there not something abnor- is there not something not quite – I mean, is there not something unusual about that?"

There was a long pause. Marianne took a book out of her bag, fingered it as if to open it, did not, and finally said quietly, "The word you were trying to avoid is *abnormal*. But what is abnormal, and what is normal? Is the world normal? Is what has happened in this century normal? Maybe it is. Normality is a chamber of horrors. I begin with wanting to express something else – the knowledge in the statue's face – and then horror takes over, because there is so much horror, and knowledge is always – though not of course entirely – the knowledge that horror exists. I don't know quite how to say any of it really, so that's how it comes out." Now she did open the book and began to leaf through it. "Simone Weil says something – I can't find it now – about sin being proportionate to the amount of light in your soul, so if you have much light and then do something evil, you are the guiltier. But it's all terribly complicated and I'm never quite sure how much I understand. If you read Simone Weil..."

"Yes, yes, I will. On your recommendation. But I want to come back to you. I grant we have a world full of horrors, but why are you obsessed with that statue, and why does that obsession make you incapable of doing simple work you have done very well in the past? Is nothing else – your credit for the course, or the purpose of your coming here – important any more?"

"But I am doing the work. I've handed you a story full of culture clash. Doesn't it make a point about old France and young America? Why can't the point be in narrative form?"

Well, why in fact could it not? Defeated, Robert said, "Okay, I'll try to explain to the administration. You know all these papers have to be passed on. But I can't help feeling there is something troubling you, something more than just the general awfulness of the world, that the statue maybe signifies something in your own life, something that you might need help in dealing with…"

"No." Marianne got up. "No, nothing else is troubling me. Have you ever seen the statue?"

"Yes, as I've seen the rest of the cathedral. I can't say it made a particular impression."

"Look at it again then." And with that, clutching Simone Weil, she left.

Robert had to report his failure to the head, who remarked, "She's reading Simone Weil? Simone Weil is not good for them. I knew of one who became a nun… unless it's the other way around and it's the nutters who tend to go for that kind of obscure modern mysticism."

"I think, though, that maybe I should look again at the statue," Robert said. But he did not, because shortly after that the summer course on French Civilisation ended in a flurry of pairings and break-ups, two engagements, one serious scandal (a tutor, female, caught in bed with a student, also female), and Marianne Laubfeld, who had begun spending nights away from her room, was twice found hiding in the cathedral after closing hours, and sent home under a worse cloud than that of sexual misconduct – the cloud of a psychotic breakdown.

## II

Letter from Marianne Laubfeld to Robert North

Dear Mr North (or should I now say Professor – you were, weren't you, on your way to a Ph.D.?)

I wrote this last story – it will be the last – on the advice of one of my therapists, Dr Millmoss (I call them all Dr Millmoss, that being the man whose hat is all that's left after he's been eaten by a big beast in the Thurber cartoon – you know, the one with the caption 'What Have You Done With Dr Millmoss?' I don't think they appreciate it.) Sorry, I ramble on – I guess it's these pills they give me. I don't concentrate very well.

Anyway, I think the idea of the story, the new story, is to show them I'm cured (three years is a long time to spend in and out of loony bins), and I thought I would send it to you, since you were so critical of the first two, and it kind of completes the series.

Don't ask me what the loony bins were like. Since my parents are rich mine were probably about as good as it gets, so I shouldn't complain.

Actually, it wasn't only the statue I thought about that summer. Did you ever guess that I wanted quite badly to sleep with you? I've told the Drs Millmoss about that, too; it makes me sound more normal. (All the girls wanted to sleep with you, but I suppose you knew that.)

Good luck and happiness and success in whatever you do and I promise I won't bother you again,

Sincerely yours,
Marianne Laubfeld

*Sacred And Profane*

Once upon a time there was a very pretty but flighty girl whose shallow and superficial parents, hoping to give her a patina of culture and so a higher value on the marriage market, sent her to France.

In France she stood out among the bird-brained young ladies at her finishing school for her insolence to her teachers and her daring midnight exploits. She even managed to vamp the waiter from the local expensive hotel and hide him in her room for three days. There the girls fed him chocolate and oranges and an aphrodisiac they wheedled from the nearest pharmacy, and a grand orgy was had by all. The waiter lost his job and never found another, but had a spectacular story to tell the other *clochards* who sat around with him under bridges smoking butts picked up in the street and brewing stolen coffee in abandoned cans. He was to tell this story from one end of France to the other, for many years, until his gums were toothless and his tongue would hardly move in his alcohol-fuzzed mouth.

One of the other girls dared Annie Marie Laurie – that was her parents' fanciful name for this daring little broad – to spend the night in the town's cathedral, where there was a statue which local legend said would walk at midnight and claim any girl it might meet for a bride. The idea of a night in the cathedral was really frightening and the others all chimed in, not averse to seeing Annie perhaps taken down a peg or two. "Betcha won't do it, Annie," they chorused. One of the more sensitive added anxiously, however, "I certainly wouldn't do it. I could pee from fright just thinking about it."

"Nothing to it," said Annie. "You just watch my steam." And she got herself well equipped for a night in the cold cathedral, with a thermos of hot chocolate, with food, cognac, chewing gum, her favourite teddy bear, and heaven knows what else. She also took a hammer – just in case, she said, the marble guy got a little too fresh.

Then Annie waved goodbye to her friends at the churchyard gate, bribed the sacristan extravagantly to let her stay after hours to spend the night in prayer for the departed soul of her dear dead grandmother, and prepared for her vigil.

After spreading out all her supplies on a pew as if it were a picnic table, she mooched over in her Ferragamo wedgies to have a look at this stone man who threatened to make her his bride.

She saw a reclining figure in long robes, holding a sword and with a lion at its feet. His face was neither young nor old, neither warrior's nor saint's, and yet it could have been any or all of those things. It was a face in which sensuality had been honed into asceticism, courage and passion and rage into the ironic wisdom and detachment of age. The smile of the statue was beautiful, inscrutable, and strange, for this king smiled like the great Buddhas, and had Annie known how to look for it, she might have found the secret of all history and all holiness hidden in that smile. But she didn't. However, she did think him not a bad looking guy.

She sat down beside him, watching him attentively. "Well, old boy," she said cheerfully, not too loudly because the cathedral did echo in a rather spooky way, "I guess you are I are alone for the night." Just for good measure she lit another couple of candles by the statue's head; then she uncorked her thermos, had a good wide yawn, and opened a magazine.

There are three possible endings to this story.

In the first, morning will find the statue vanished, and Annie mutilated and dead. In the second, the statue will be smashed to pieces, and Annie tapping the floor with a blood-soaked hammer and keening to herself, crazy as a hoot-owl, her lovely red hair gone white.

But the third one is a lot more likely.

The sacristan, a bit apprehensive, unlocks the cathedral door. The musty damp darkness rushes out at him. He is guilty and regretful; handsome tip or not, he shouldn't really have left anyone here overnight. That crazy American, where can she be? There she is, sprawled out sacrilegiously on one of the pews, sound asleep. Prayer and vigil indeed! He taps her indignantly on the shoulder. Annie yawns, grumbles, stretches, and begins to gather her things together. Then, after a last quick glance at the marble man on the slab, she hurries out to collect her winnings.

And the moral, if you want one, is this.

With money and an empty head

You walk where angels fear to tread

And the statue?

The statue still smiles his inscrutable smile.

❀     ❀     ❀

Robert North, then a busy man involved in the final work on his thesis, and in a serious love affair that was beginning to go wrong, put this letter aside in a pile of others to be answered when time allowed. It would need much time, much thought, and much tact; it was not an easy letter to answer. He did not put it aside, however, without a twinge of conscience and a twinge of regret. *Did you ever guess that I wanted quite badly to sleep with you?* Did she ever guess, had it not been for the student-teacher situation with its dangers and restraints... but no, thank heaven he had avoided that danger. Being involved with psychotics, curable or not, was not a happy choice.

Whether Marianne was curable or not would never be decided. A few weeks after sending her letter to Robert North, ostensibly 'quite well again and full of hope and plans and promise', her tearful parents were quoted as saying, Marianne was dead.

"Overdose," said one of Robert's former summer seminar colleagues, with whom he discussed the news. They had both received funeral notices, having been prominent in Marianne's address book. "God knows how she got enough of the stuff. I know a doctor at her last clinic (*one of the Millmosses*, Robert thought, *she probably ran rings around them*). They had no reason to think she was suicidal. She never tried suicide before, nor ever mentioned it. But my friend said her appearance of improvement is quite typical; suicides, having made up their minds, can be quite calm and cheerful, make an optimistic impression. Didn't you say you had quite an up-beat sounding letter from her?"

"Yes. Yes, I did." Robert had more than a twinge of conscience now. *I promise I won't bother you again.* Were the letter and the story a last minute call for help – was he the person she had chosen to guide her out of her labyrinth, if it were possible? Or was there a last message she wanted someone – no, *him* – to receive from her?

*Why didn't I write?* He thought over and over, *why did I not at least acknowledge the letter, why did I do nothing until it was too late?* He promised himself that soon he would go back to Perpignan and look at that royal tomb; if there was a message he might, after all, find it there. He owed that to Marianne. But whatever he did, he felt that Marianne, haunted by her statue, would haunt him until the day he died.

Marianne, of course, did not really haunt him for long. His serious affair soon ended, leaving Robert himself depressed and listless, and with something more intimate to haunt him, until he made a rebound but reasonably happy marriage, fathered two children, and progressed up the academic ladder in what could justifiably be called a very successful career. *Good luck and happiness and success in whatever you do.* So it was many years later, now retired, a widower, a grandfather, and perhaps soon to be a great-grandfather, that Robert, remembering his ancient promise and thinking he must fulfill it while still able to travel, found himself once more in Perpignan.

Perpignan was a very different place. Much bigger, much spruced up, but also somehow more blemished, with the seediness of modernity, with package tourists snapping photos on their new-generation mobile phones, or making videos of motionless objects, with fast food and too many cars, with third-world immigrants whose faces were sullen with deprivation as many of the faces of just post World War II Europe had been in a time no one seemed to want to recall. There had been a magic here, he thought, in spite of the poverty; sunlight through green shutters, leafy courtyards, somnolent cafés, a sense of space. France still had more space than most, but space was vanishing in the overcrowded, exhausted world. He smiled to himself, turning over the thought. *Shutter, somnolent, sense, space.* Too much alliteration.

Shuffling and hesitant – his eyes were no longer so good, nor his legs – Robert entered the cathedral. At first the murky, scented darkness overwhelmed him; then he saw the statue, surrounded by candles, and a person bent over it. A boy still in his teens, and judging by his T-shirt and jeans, his haircut, his scrubbed, fair, slightly overfed look, an American boy. Then Robert remembered. Now they all dressed the same, looked nearly the same. It was only in matching a crowd of one nation against a crowd of another that differences were still visible. If even then.

"Shit," the boy said out loud. "Whoops – I'm in church. Sorry, whoever heard that," he politely addressed the darkness. "I just can't get this right."

Robert, moving closer, saw the boy was holding a drawing pad and that there were pieces of paper scattered around the statue and on nearby pews. Seeing Robert, whom he obviously thought a local or even someone connected to the cathedral, the boy added quickly in French, "*Je vais ramasser tout ça. Toute suite.*" I'll pick it all up, right away.

Robert came still closer with his faltering old man's step. "It's okay," he said. "I'm just a tourist. And you – you're drawing the statue."

"Yah. I'm an art student. I'm here on a summer programme. I've got kind of obsessed with this statue. Specially the way it looks in candlelight. That's why I buy all the candles. I'm almost running out of candle money, and the church people are complaining about my being here so much. But I made this my project and I have to finish it. There's something I want to get in the statue's face, something weird, I can't explain it, something you see maybe in Buddha faces, something in the smile. Only not Buddha faces either, not quite... but I have to get it. My teachers hate what I'm doing, they just want concept art, installations and stuff, that's the only thing they think is cool anymore. They're beginning to think I'm kind of crazy, coming here day after day, drawing this same hunk of marble over and over again. But I don't want to leave here until I've got it."

"No," Robert said. "I don't think you're crazy. But I think you may become so if you go on. I think it will destroy you." What was it Marianne had said – *a knowledge after which nothing is possible except death.* "There was a girl here – one of my students, many years ago..."

And in a tremulous voice he told the boy Marianne's story. The boy hardly listened. After a brief flash of interest, he was concentrating on yet another sketch.

"So," Robert finished, "please, please leave the statue alone. This obsession will harm you. Please believe what I say, and go."

"Not a chance," said the boy, now annoyed and aggressive.

"Okay, then. May I at least just give you my card? Would you keep in touch with me and let me know how you get on?"

"Sure," the boy said, reluctantly pocketing the card. *It's this old coot who is off his rocker*, he thought, and as soon as Robert's back was turned the boy put the card with is rejected sketches to throw away. As for Robert, he stumbled back outside, too upset to realize that he had not even fulfilled his promise; he had been so concerned with the obsessed young artist he had not really looked at the statue's face.

❋ ❋ ❋

Who then was Sanche, King of Majorca, who sleeps under his effigy and will sleep still, long after that effigy may have vanished in a new chaos, the likely end of this age that heralds the planet's exhaustion and the culminating self-indulgence of the greedy prolific human race?

In 1324 he laid the foundation stone of the cathedral where he lies and because of which he is chiefly remembered. He died soon after, having lived about fifty years. Few other facts are readily available, but it seems he was a decent and peaceable king. As kings go. I discovered one interesting incident regarding his reign; when he besieged a rebellious town, he tried in vain the stop his troops from committing the slaughter, rape, and pillage they considered their due. Or perhaps he did not try hard enough. This was all found in an outdated encyclopedia, and I have never been able to find King Sanche's story again, not even through the wondrous mechanisms of our electronic era. With so much new information about, much old information gets lost in the shuffle; or, perhaps, wanting an explanation for the strange quality of that marble face, I only imagined the reference and the book.

# Grandmother Wolf

" ... And standing by a window a girl said:
'Only once I saw one, once, once;
Far out over the snow, in a hard winter –
When I was a little girl, at our country place.
And Anya, our old nurse said: 'Look, child –
Come to the window, and I will show you a wolf.'
(For often the long evenings she had told us of them)
And there it went, the lonely one, like a great dog –
But hindquarters narrow and drooping, like a cowardly
dog –
Hungry nose to the snow, onward, onward.
But sometimes it paused, and scraped in its tracks, and
raised
Its great head to the bitter skies, and howled.

... And the black-browed girl by the window said,
remembering
'Always in my dreams it is thus, always in my dreams
Snow and moonlight, snow and the dark pines
moaning,
Fur over my body, and my feet small,
Delicate and swift to run through the powdery snow,
And my sharp mouth to the ground, hungry, hungry,
And always onward, onward, alone, alone ...

Moon, moon, cold mouth over the pine-trees,
Or are you hunting me, or I pursuing?' "

Two stanzas from *Valse Oubliée* by John Heath-Stubbs
from his book *The Charity of the Stars,*
William Sloane Inc. NY 1949
*Author's Note:* This poem has always haunted me, and
I finally decided to invent a life for the "black-browed
girl by the window" – hence this story.

They cannot pronounce her name. They call her Tatty.

Her name is Tatiana Varvara, and in all the years she has lived among English speakers she has never allowed Tatiana to become Tanya, though now there are many English Tanyas, just as there are Natashas and Laras, and using Tanya would have made things easier. When the staff at the nursing home ask Tatiana to please eat a little of her soup – "Oh please, Tatty. Just a teeny spoonful. For your grand-daughter. For Nina," or when they say "Please Tatty, let go," as she twists the big blue plastic bib in her twisted fingers and dunks it in the soup, she does not respond.

But then she no longer responds to anything much. Anything outside her own body. Anything outside her own mind.

Malka, the Polish care attendant, who could say Tatiana or even Madame Raminovsky, the maiden name Tatiana went back to after her long-ago divorce, does not wish to call attention to herself by doing so. They might think she was putting on airs. It is hard enough that the other girl from Eastern Europe, the Latvian one, has told them all about Malka's degree in literature. "Why ain't you teaching then? What are you doing here, wiping bums?"

The Latvian girl has contempt for degrees. She is a farm girl, very big, very strong. She is good at getting patients in and out of chairs, beds, baths and off the floor when they fall, but there is something not very gentle about the way she does it. Malka is a little afraid of her.

"She doesn't want to see the doctor any more," Nurse Barnes says to Tatiana's grand-daughter Nina. "And the last time we took her blood pressure it needed two of us, one to hold her down. She hates anyone touching her. We do our best, we try to keep her clean, but it's hard."

"I'm sure you do your best," Nina answers, a phrase she has used often before.

"She's incredibly strong for someone of a hundred. She really is amazing for that age."

"She might even be older. Her family lost all their papers when they left Russia. But from what she used to tell us when she still talked, at least a hundred. She remembers a big place in the country and they lost that before she was eight. They lost everything in the Revolution, and her father was killed. The women were lucky to escape with their lives."

Nina has repeated this story to each new matron and each nurse – there seems to be a fair turnover – in the fifteen years her grandmother has been at Chy Simpering. She hopes it will get Granny sympathetic treatment. Sometimes the staff were curious and wanted stories of Granny's past. But what had Granny ever told the family about Russia, except the story of the wolf in the snow?

"It never ends, does it, asylum seekers," says Nurse Barnes. "I guess she *was* pretty lucky. But now there's too many. You can't take in everyone. And some of them just fake it."

"Most of them don't, I think. Most people don't really want to leave their own countries. But yes, she was lucky." She looks at the meagre figure in the wheelchair and thinks, not lucky now.

Since it has been decided that she is a hundred, Tatiana is in fact getting treatment as sympathetic as Chy Simpering is able to give. It is a feather in their cap to have a hundred-year-old patient, though that age is not nearly as rare as it was even a decade ago. And if they could keep her going for a few more years – maybe even to 105? Already last year there was the birthday telegram from the Queen. It means nothing to poor

Tatty of course, she doesn't seem to understand a word they say any more. However, it means something to the staff. They have framed the telegram and put it up in the hall by the visitor's entrance. It's their first one but they hope for more. There's old Josiah Tamworth, he's 97 and seems in pretty good shape. He might make it. And jolly Millie Belforn, 96 and still going strong in spite of being overweight.

The wolf Tatiana saw was at their family estate. The last time they were ever there for Christmas. The last time they were ever to see that beloved place again.

Perhaps that was why the memory was so vivid. There was not much to it really. Her nanny called her to the window to see a wolf, a lone wolf skulking at the edge of the forest. Little Tatiana watched, enraptured, the great dark beast snuffling and scratching the snow and then raising his head to howl, as if the human world, the people behind the lighted windows not far away, did not exist. At last with a sudden bound he was gone among the trees.

The wolf grew in Tatiana's mind until he was as big as a lion. But it was much later, after her beloved father's death and when they were exiles in Paris, that Tatiana's dreams began.

"Would you like chocolate, Granny?"
"You used to like chocolate, Granny."
"Or grapes, Granny? You used to love grapes."

They don't call her Great-granny because that is too long and complicated. Behind her back they call her Great-great because it sounds like that funny noise she sometimes makes in her throat, which makes them giggle, though they try to restrain themselves.

The children put the grapes and chocolate on the messy table in front of her, wrinkling their noses a little because she does smell (why do old people have to smell like that), a personal smell which cuts through the general odour of urine and carbolic and cabbage long boiled. Their mother Nina quickly picks up the grapes and chocolate before the old woman can push them off the table. These abrupt gestures of rejection and refusal are the only gestures Tatiana still makes.

"We'll put them aside for her. Maybe she'll eat them later," Nina says.

To her family as to the staff, the old woman, having reached a hundred – that age at which it is surely possible to discard at last the stupid euphemism of 'elderly' and say simply 'old' – has become a bit less of a burden and more an object of interest. Even Nina's very English husband occasionally accompanies Nina on her visits and says a few hearty words in the direction of Granny's large wrinkled ears. "You'll outlive us all, Granny," he says.

Superstitious Nina, hearing this, says a silent prayer. Please God not. She looks at the motionless figure in the wheelchair, the big felt slippers jutting like toadstools from under the lap rug, the claw hands that sometimes spontaneously curl against the thin chest, making Granny look like a grotesque stick insect, a praying mantis. Please God not. And then she thinks, but what really do *I* have to live for, I am so often so tired, so tired, tired of this jovial man and these alien children who care for nothing I really am and nothing I know and are now clamouring, please Mummy can we go, please Mummy can I put my gameboy on, please Mummy we want to go home and watch that new video Daddy got. You said we could if we went with you today. Mummy, you said. And then Nina thinks no, no, what is wrong with me, of course I love the children, I have to stop thinking what Roger calls my dark Russian thoughts.

The nurses fed Tatiana weak soups and watery porridge, meat with a texture like damp cardboard, fish smelling not of sea but of decay, glutinous pudding tasting of cheap candy, with a cherry in the middle whose very colour made her retch. She longed for the rich tastes of her youth, for wild mushrooms and *shashlik* and thick sour cream, for the pickled garlic and chillies they had with vodka, for always she could down the same strong stuff as her male relatives and she could drink with them like a man. Now food is indifferent to her; she has almost stopped eating. Yet she still longs for a taste she cannot place at once metallic and strangely sweet.

When they still tried to feed her solid food, again and again she threw her spoon on the floor like an angry child. One day the Latvian woman forced a spoon between her teeth and hurt her, and then she did taste blood. Her own.

The Latvian woman was reprimanded and after that for a while they left her alone, and then began feeding her only liquid nutritional formula. She takes some of that because she still craves liquid. However, they do not tell Nina; they tell Nina that she does eat, but just not when she is excited, not when the family is there.

Tatiana grew up in France still speaking mostly Russian, the language her mother and aunt continued to speak at home. Paris after the Revolution was full of White Russian refugees, many of them with poignant memories of their estates, some with poignant memories of estates they never had. Loss was always part of refugees' luggage, even if it was, like some of their titles, acquired at the frontier.

Tatiana was sent to school and quickly learned French but remained a lonely child. She did not make friends easily. She was shy and distant, inhibited by the contrast between her life at school and her home life in a shabby apartment where mysterious relations came and went, clustering around the samovar and occupying any spare sleeping space so Tatiana had to sleep in a little bed in her mother's room. At school she mostly sat with another Russian girl, who Tatiana had begun to hope was a best as well as an only friend. One day in a burst of confidence she told this friend her favourite memory, the story of the wolf.

To Tatiana's surprise the other girl drew herself up and said haughtily, "One wolf? You only ever saw one wolf? We had many wolves in the wood at *our* estate. They even killed two of the peasants. And my nanny told me they ran in packs and sometimes they would chase troikas, and in the snow they were faster than the horses, and once a family threw out a baby to slow the wolves down."

"Threw out a baby?" Tatiana was incredulous.

"They had to. Or they would all have been eaten," said the other girl sensibly. "Anyway, they were all only peasants. My family carried guns when they went out in winter and my father and uncle shot many wolves. We have a wolf-skin rug. Would you like to see it?"

"No," Tatiana answered without hesitation, though it was the first invitation from a schoolmate she had ever had. Then she went on musingly, "I wonder what that would taste like. To eat a baby."

The friend looked hard at Tatiana, her white even teeth, her thick dark eyebrows, her glossy back hair. She said nothing. But the next day she asked to sit next to someone else and she never spoke to Tatiana again.

"I don't think you should go so often," Roger says to Nina in the car driving home. "It depresses you. And what does it do for her? She doesn't even recognise you any more."

"She is angry," Nina says. "She chooses not to recognise us. She is still angry with us all for putting her in that horrible place."

Roger sighs. "It's not a horrible place. It's the best we could have found." He does not add; and I, who am not strictly speaking even related to the dear old virago, am paying through the nose for it. "She can't still be angry after fifteen years. Anyway, they say old people die quickly in care homes. Quicker than at home. She's fifteen years there and a hundred old and still going. If she were so miserable or badly cared for would she still be alive?"

"I don't think she wants to be alive. There is something that won't let her go. Or maybe it's as if when you get past a certain age life is like a bad habit you don't have the will to get rid of. Like smoking or drugs. As if you're too old and feeble to have the will to die."

"Dying doesn't take will. Suicide takes will. Dying is what happens in spite of you."

"It's not that simple," Nina says.

"If I were Granny I would want to die," says Billy from the back, "sitting in a chair all day not talking and getting smelly."

"I thought you were on the gameboy," Roger says. Then to Nina, "I think we should have this conversation later."

Nina goes on musing half to herself, ignoring them both. "And also they won't let you die. Not easily. Or maybe –" Nina hesitates, "Maybe it's as if she's still waiting for something."

This, thinks Roger with exasperation, is Nina's usual nonsense, her fucking Slavic mysticism she still carries around in the third generation. Thank God the other relations are long gone and my kids are not being addled with all the stuff about vast estates and icons and troikas in the snow. Though it wouldn't mean anything to them anyway. Disney and robots and the play-station is what they're into. Computer whizzes already, his kids. He is proud of them.

"What could you be waiting for, at age one hundred?"

"It's not rational," says Nina irritably and then to Billy, "For God's sake, I can't stand that noise. Turn the gameboy down."

"That story about throwing a baby out of the sled is a stupid legend peasants tell," said Aunt Nadjezda. "What did you say the girl's name was – Kulminov? Hah, I know the family. They had a little factory. No forests, no wolves. They would never have been invited where your parents were. The stupid girl was trying to impress you."

"But when they are starving wolves will eat people," Tatiana's mother put in. "And people will eat people. Anyone will eat anything."

"Yes, and people eat wolves. Which reminds me that we have Count Belinski coming this evening and we must get something together for supper." Then to her sister in a low voice, "Your child is already upset. Why do you tell her such things?"

That night Tatiana dreamed her wolf dream. Only in this dream she was not trotting through the white wilderness and then raising her head to howl at the bitter winter moon. She was nosing at a little whimpering bundle left in the snow. She felt its face, already cold, against her nose. She licked the face. The thing whimpered more. She began to undo its wrappings with her teeth, spitting out hairs from the strange fur covering.

Then, shaking with terror, she woke up.

In this county where it almost never snows, the staff still go out in shirt-sleeves to smoke their cigarettes, and some of the more appreciative old are still wheeled once round the garden on a sunny winter day. It is a long time since anyone has taken Tatiana, who is not appreciative of anything, out of the cabbage-carbolic fug, out into the air.

Tatiana can no longer make sentences in her head but a few words remain, along with images and sensations, or memories of sensations and sounds and feelings and smells. And questions, no longer verbal, only a nameless impulse or an undefined need. What was it when the moon rose full and the black shadows of the trees lay long and sharp on the snow at the forest's edge? The moon is shut out by the multi-coloured curtains, prints that match the carpet pattern selected so as not to reveal vomit stains. But a little of the moonlight comes through.

The smokers on the terrace, having a break, are betting whether Tatty will make a hundred and one. Matron angrily summons them inside. There is Mr Brace who needs toileting, Miss Cavendish slumped half out of her chair, Mr Dearborn calling for water, Mr Penfold calling for help. This new matron does not know that Mr Penfold calls for help every Friday but why this is no one knows nor does anyone know what Mr Penfold requires.

It was after her new dream that the child Tatiana asked a question she had never, for some reason, thought to ask before; why she had no brother or sister.

Her mother said embarrassedly, "When you were born it was very difficult. And then – your father saw that bad times would come – and then of course we lost him –" Tatiana was satisfied with this explanation but her mother, after a few tears, continued. "And there was something else wrong. When you were born they found something else growing that was – like a twin, but that never became a real baby. It was just – it had hair. Little bones and hair. The doctor thought perhaps it was better for me not to have more children."

"Why on earth are you telling her this horror? It was nothing, just a growth. A benign growth," said Aunt Nadjezda coming in.

"No, I shouldn't have told you, Tatiana, I'm sorry. Would you have liked a sister or brother?"

"No," said Tatiana, greatly relieved. She did not want a small brother or sister. She had made the remark about the taste of babies only to shock her friend whose boasts about wolf-hunting had infuriated her. But her dream had left her very frightened and the story of the strange tumour-twin made her doubly glad that even if her mother ever married again, as her friend Princess Lubomirska had, there could be no sequel. For what was it that had almost been? Hair and bones. A baby wolf. Not a child at all.

Tonight old Tatty is restless. She not only twists her big blue plastic bib, she tears it, with surprising energy. These bibs are getting expensive enough, what with the price of oil, that soon unless they are really soiled the staff may be forced to use them several times, hanging them over the backs of the chairs between meals but not when visitors can see. With another bout of energy Tatty spits out her nutritional formula and her water. Mr Penfold calls for help loudly all through dinner. Miss Cavendish falls right out of her chair. Bobby Harefield, with his mouth full of mashed potato, begins to sing. It is a bad night.

By the time Tatiana was a young woman the family finances had improved and Tatiana herself changed from a frail bony girl, awkward and too tall, into a beauty. Her face was vivid and expressive and she had a mocking way of wrinkling her nose when she was disdainful of something, as she often was, that her mother and aunt considered vulgar but men found very provocative. Her figure was perfect and in spite of the depressed economy she readily found work modelling in Paris boutiques. She met and was propositioned by a number of men. She did not accept the propositions. She wanted proposals. In due course at a dance she met a young French nobleman who listened with fascination to Tatiana's memory of the wolf in the snow and how those vast glittering fields and the lone dark animal raising his head to the moon had haunted her all through her childhood. A few months later he married her. Five years later he was dead from a rare blood disorder, leaving large debts which Tatiana could not pay.

"Help," calls old Harry Penfold again. He bangs his spoon against his cup. A few others imitate him, making some kind of sound with their cutlery.

Why is it always on a Friday, wonders Malka. Maybe the fish they have on Friday does not agree with him, does something to his stomach. Though he always eats it. Old Harry is one of the few who always eats.

In the dining room now there is a cacophony of noise; cutlery, belches, groans, exclamations, farts and the rustling plastic bibs and also of course the coaxing and scolding of nurses. It is like feeding babies, thinks the Latvian girl, big ugly babies, how I hate them, I will try again for the supermarket job, they have to let me, I am in the EU. They have no right to take the Cornish people first. She is big and strong, she would be a better shelf-stacker any day than those mincing creatures with hair in corkscrews and rings in their noses like a prize bull.

When the Germans occupied France Tatiana no

longer thought of wolves or even of noblemen. The family was intent only on survival. They moved in with relations in a small country town; they lived precariously, from mother Ludmilla's music lessons which she often bartered for produce, from Nadjezda's sewing, from any work Tatiana could get. They kept chickens and rabbits. It was Tatiana and her aunt who killed them, Nadjezda expertly breaking the rabbits' necks, Tatiana cutting off the chickens' heads. Ludmilla could not even bear to watch. One day a British airman was found concealed behind their rabbit hutches. They managed to hide him until the Allied invasion.

This soldier was the second man Tatiana married. The marriage did not last long. It ended in divorce only three years later, soon after Tatiana had a son. Tatiana was not good with babies or children. The son was soon sent to boarding school and spent most of his holidays with his father.

Left comfortably off, Tatiana remained in England on her own. While her mother and aunt still lived, she made frequent trips to France. Later she became more and more a recluse, alone in her house on the moors with her dogs. She had always coveted dogs but had never liked her first husband's birding spaniels which she had not considered proper dogs at all. Tatiana wanted something special, and now she was able to indulge herself. She imported a rare breed of fawn-coloured black-muzzled sheepdogs and bred them, selling them at high prices to carefully selected customers. This venture was actually quite successful and the eccentric figure of Tatiana striding across the moors with two or three of her big powerful beasts became a sight her village was proud of, though still slightly uncomfortable with. Occasionally a dog escaped and killed sheep but Tatiana paid for the sheep so handsomely, never quibbling about either the deed or the prices, that it was said there were farmers who deliberately let a sheep stray on her land.

When Tatiana's son married she did not even attend the wedding. In spite of this parental neglect, when his daughter Nina was four, her son decided to bring her to meet her grandmother. They took to each other at once and more surprisingly so did Nina and the dogs that so terrified Nina's mother she would not go near the house. With frequent visits from Nina Tatiana continued alone and independent until her dementia began.

With the dementia her dreams came back.

"I don't think she's got long, old Tatty," says Nurse Barnes to Nurse Jim.

"I hope she does have a bit longer. You know for all the shit in her pants Tatty is a lady. We don't have many around these days."

"You're an old-fashioned sexist," says Nurse Barnes indignantly. "A lady? What a lot of codswallop. No one with shit in their pants is a lady any more. Nor maybe ever was. Anyway the poor old thing wants to go. That's what she used to say when she was still talking. When can I go. I want to go. Over and over again. Then she began to talk in Russian, I guess it was Russian, when she talked at all."

Jim blushes. He feels a bit guilty. The reason he wants Tatiana to live is because of Nina's visits. He thinks Nina is beautiful. He is convinced Nina is unhappily married. They shared a smoke during Nina's visit the other day and he heard Nina's husband will soon be off on a business conference. Her children of course are at school all day. Taking another drag on his roll-up – there is just a very little other stuff in it – he begins to fantasise. She could get a baby-sitter one evening. Or he could go to her house on his day off. He would bring flowers. What was it she said she liked? Roses are not cool and cost too much. Chrysanthemums. Or are they somehow elderly-type flowers, would they be not complimentary for an older woman? A mixed bouquet of something ... He takes another drag and suddenly conjures up a very vivid image of Nina's breasts.

It was Nina who'd said the lady thing. Please take very good care of my grandmother. She's a lady.

Indeed a funny old-fashioned thing to say.

"Hey you two smokers, have you finished your sodding fags? Old Jessie has piddled on the floor again and it's not my sodding turn to sodding clean it up." This from Nurse Joe, the other young male carer. He's plain and full of acne, wouldn't have a chance with anyone like Nina, but he fancies her too. Fancies any woman who still has control of her bladder, thinks Jim, "Coming," he says.

"You wish," says Nurse Barnes. She has noticed his dreamy expression and the way he eyes Nina.

"In the midst of death we are in life," Jim adds cheerfully to Nurse Barnes.

"Too clever by half is what you are," Nurse Barnes as usual says back. "And since when do you call this living?"

That evening a freak bout of weather sets in. It snows heavily all night and well on into the next day.

In senile dementia the nouns go first. Give me the thing, Tatiana would say to Nina. That was when Nina knew something was going wrong. Later other words go and even the dearest proper names.

If Tatiana could still think in words they would right now be the words for a baffled and resentful wonder. Where are the rings on my hands? There were once many rings. Why do I have nothing to eat, nothing I crave, nothing to gnaw, nothing ...

Tatiana salivates and Jim wipes her mouth. Now it is

not the lost word rings she is thinking of. She is still looking at her hands but thinking of something else that is wrong, something else about her hands. Her hands are bony and hairless. It is not her rings she is missing now. What has happened to what she can walk on, what would carry her silently over the snow?

When you are so old you are on your own and sometimes the pack will kill you. Tatiana does not know this but an instinctive fear makes her heart jump in her chest. She looks around at nurses giggling in a corner, at the other gurgling talking shouting simpering creatures making alien sounds. They smell of danger. She must get away from them. Must get away. Her hands grip the wheels of the chair but the chair does not move.

"I don't like the way she looks tonight," says the Latvian girl. "She gives me the crips"

"You mean creeps," says Malka gently. "She's harmless, look at her, she can't move." Though the Latvian girl gives *her* the creeps she cannot stop herself from correcting her English. She would like to correct the English staff sometimes but manages to restrain herself.

"What you know," says the Latvian girl contemptuously. "You have degree, you say right words, but you know nothing."

At bedtime the snow-clouds clear and the moon comes up over the trees. "Night-night," says Jim and tucks Tatiana in. When they're this far gone and you're short-staffed you don't worry much about which sex looks after which. They never worried, did they, about female nurses looking after men. And of course some of the old biddies get a charge out of it. Even out of Joe. Bet Joe does too, desperate as he is with his acne.

It is dark now. The human lights are gone. There is only the cold white light, the familiar light, the light that calls. Tatiana's breath in the cold is like the breath from the red thing that men make, the thing that jumps and frightens and burns, like the breath from the other things men have that crash and wound. But now again she can feel the cold against the pads of her feet and the winter smell of forest is sharp in her nose and the strange white light shines over everything and she is outside again, she is free.

In the morning they find Tatty's window wide open and Tatty gone.

The room is a ground floor one and the window always open a little, on Nina's instructions. "She can't bear to sleep in an airless room." No one, however, had thought Tatty still able to walk. Or even crawl. They do not have to go far to find her. She has gone on all fours through the snow, her feeble legs dragging behind her hands, her thick flannel nightgown leaving a strange trail as it caught and impeded her faltering feet. She is dead and ice-cold and there is dried blood around her mouth. "Haemorrhage," says the doctor. "The sudden cold did something to her lungs." He does not add that they might have been remiss in never checking inmates for TB after another foreign care assistant was found to be carrying the disease and rapidly dismissed.

Not that Tatty ever coughed. Or certainly not more than the others.

"Well, at least the old girl made a hundred," says Nurse Barnes. "And she did get out in the end."

Nina cries for days. Malka cries too without quite knowing why. The Latvian girl crosses herself and curses. Jim curses too; Nina will not be visiting any more. Roger breathes a sigh of relief. The care home was becoming unaffordable, the money from the sale of the last dogs and Tatiana's house on the moor long gone. He suggests a family winter break in Majorca to cheer Nina up.

Not only has Tatiana died but the girl with dreadlocks and nose-rings, last seen walking home from a club in the country on the same snowy night, is missing. The Latvian girl gets her job and is soon happily stacking shelves.

# The Saracen Girl

"Oh please Grandpa," said my cousin Trudy for the dozenth time that summer, "tell us the story of the beautiful girl in the basket and the faithful slave."

Grandfather sighed, and I did too. This was a true and very dramatic story but I thought we had heard it often enough. I myself preferred the stories of snowstorms and avalanches, of the lamb that had survived in a dead man's arms, of the buried woman who was found because her long hair stuck up above the snow, of the old man who when he was rescued unhurt from the avalanches complained that he had lost his pipe. Children like the bizarre and gruesome, as fairy tales confirm. But Trudy had become obsessed with her favourite story, and I rather wished Grandpa would not give in. Trudy's obsessions usually boded no good. However, when Trudy, who was a very winning little girl, curled up close to him and fixed large pleading blue eyes on his face, Grandpa could not resist.

"Once upon a time," he began, "there was a young maiden whose father, a knight, left his castle to fight in the crusades. Many years the family waited for him, growing poor and dejected with no man except a lazy steward to help the girl's mother run the estate. By the time the knight reappeared, the girl's two little brothers had died of a sickness from which she recovered but was left lame. The girl had grown into a beauty and learned to read and write, unusual for a girl in those long-ago days, but her lameness was looked on as a great fault and her parents feared no man of rank would ever marry her. Her father was bitterly aggrieved by the death of his sons and the state of his poor daughter. That was how it was in those distant times, children were not treasured for themselves but for what they might do and what they might bring when they came of age. You do not know how fortunate you children are."

"Please," said Trudy, "go on with the story."

"The knight did however give his daughter a gift – a little slave, a Saracen girl around her own age he had captured in the Holy Land. The little slave grew to love her mistress, whose kindness was probably the only kindness she had known since her own father, no doubt, was butchered by the crusading knights."

"Must you call it butchery?" This was from Grandma, who was quite devout while Grandpa was not.

"Butchery it was," said Grandpa firmly. "To continue. The young noblewoman taught the girl to speak the local language – French or German, I am not sure as there have been many changes of borders since – and also began to teach her to read, and protected her from the other servants who thought her an infidel without a soul and treated her badly. The little slave became more and more devoted and never left her mistress's side.

One day the father rode back to the castle in great excitement. He had heard from a neighbour – an ugly old knight who I believe had taken a fancy to the beautiful daughter, lame though she was – of a miraculous hot spring in the mountains where perhaps her lameness could be cured. And where, do you think, was the miraculous hot spring?"

"Here, of course," we chorused.

"Here, of course, where your granny and I take the baths every summer."

"But it's not miraculous really," I put in as I usually did, "it hasn't cured all your rheumatism yet or Grandma's horrid toe."

"Be quiet," said Trudy, "and let him go on."

"So they rode for many days to reach the spring, the

knight and his daughter and their servants and the old knight who also wished a cure as he was arthritic like your grandpa. They rode in fear of wolves and bears and bandits, staying in rude inns, often hungry and cold and wet, but at last they arrived. In those days there were no hotels, no bathhouse, no baths, only a hut for patients to change into a coarse woollen dress for their dipping and two men standing on opposite sides of the narrow gorge who lowered the patient in a big basket, held by ropes, into the warm pool.

For the poor lame young lady, there was no miracle. When they hauled up the basket and lifted her out she was as lame as before. So they determined to try again, and the next day they left her from morning till evening in the warm pool. She made no sound all day – or if she did they could not hear it above the rushing water. But when they finally pulled her up she was stone dead. And the little slave tried to revive her mistress, and when she saw it was in vain, she gave a great cry and leapt into the gorge. And her poor body hurtled down the stream and when it was found she was buried at the nearest crossroads, which is how they buried suicides."

"And as she was an infidel," I added sagely, "they could anyhow never have put her in consecrated ground."

"Do stop interrupting Grandpa with all your facts," said Trudy. "Go on, Grandpa. And then she became a ghost -"

"I don't know what she became but it is true that through the ages since there have been those who claimed they saw the little Saracen girl, always before a great calamity. Before the great avalanche that destroyed half this town, before Napoleon came, before the first great war and again before the second great war. But not since. But no one knows if she really has been seen -"

Grandma put in sternly, "Or if those sightings are the false recollections of superstitious peasants who wish to make themselves important. It is not wise to put frightening heathen ideas into children's heads."

"We like being frightened, Grandma," I said.

"I'm never frightened," said Trudy. "I could see the Saracen girl and not be scared at all."

My cousin Trudy and I were both only children and though we frequently quarrelled were the best of friends. Our summer mountain holidays with our Swiss grandparents, who always booked a room for us at their favourite spa hotel, were the high point of our lives. Trudy, who was nine that year, two years younger than I was, was as imaginative and fanciful as I was curious but prosaic. Where I would go for a walk with a botany book and try to identify Alpine flowers, Trudy would be looking for trolls and fairies and speaking to her imaginary friends, of whom she had a number and whom she frequently blamed for naughty deeds of her own. So it did not surprise me when one day Trudy, having gone off by herself – in our childhood we had much more liberty than children do now – came back breathless and told me she had a great secret for me. "Don't ever tell Grandpa and Grandma. We're never supposed to go up to the gorge without them. But I did. I wanted to see the Saracen girl. And I did."

"Trudy, you're lying."

"I am not lying. I saw her. She was on top of the rocks. She was dressed in those puffy trousers and she had a gauze veil and red slippers with long curled-up toes -"

"You are absolutely lying. You're just describing a picture in Grandpa's French story book, the one by Pierre Lotto."

"Pierre Loti," said Trudy, proving she had looked at it more recently than I.

"The poor girl would never be dressed like that. She was a slave, remember? And people only see her when something dreadful is going to happen. You wouldn't want to see her even if you could."

"Dreadful things were maybe just in old times." Trudy was unshaken. "I know I saw her. I'll prove it. If you come with me you'll see her too."

"All right, I'll come. Just this once. Just to prove what a silly liar you are." I was angry at her stubborn insistence, and I knew I could not stop her going to the gorge again, unless I told our grandparents and got us both confined to the garden.

"Right now," cried Trudy. "Granny and Grandpa are in the baths, they won't miss us. Let's go right now."

We took the path up along the stream, Trudy running ahead, scrambling over roots and rocks, agile as a chamois. At last we came to the big boulders that leaned over the stream from both banks and only a few feet apart, from where the patients in baskets had been lowered into the warm pool below.

"Trudy," I shouted, "don't go near the edge."

"I won't. We'll just sit here and wait. You'll see – she'll just suddenly be there, on the other side."

And so we waited, until the sun was touching the great crags of the mountain above us and a chill came into the air and mist rose from the pool below.

"Trudy," I said, "we'll be late for supper, we have to go now."

"Just another few minutes," Trudy pleaded.

"No. This is crazy. If we're late they'll be angry and won't let us out alone. And you know we're not supposed to be up here at all."

"Okay," said Trudy sadly but then, brightening up, "If we hurry we can go past the bridge where we can play Pooh-sticks." And before I could protest that this way back would take longer, she was running down the path at a pace I could not match. When I reached the bridge, out of breath and annoyed, Trudy was hopping up and down, two nice fat sticks ready in her hands. "There's yours and here's mine. Come on, just one game."

We dropped our sticks and waited. "That's mine," cried Trudy, "mine's ahead -" Then she broke off and clutched my arm. "Oh my God," said Trudy. "Oh my God, oh my God. Look what's coming - under the bridge -"

And then I saw it, and like Trudy who still clutched my arm hard enough to bruise it, I stood transfixed, for emerging from under the bridge was a body in a long ragged dress, a body so battered its face was beyond recognition, a hideous mass of broken bones and long tangled dark hair, and as we watched the body jammed against rocks and one arm was flung up as if pointing at us.

"Someone's fallen in -" I finally managed to gasp, "we have to run and tell Grandpa -"

"No," said Trudy in a strangely hushed voice. "No one fell, not now. Don't you know who it is?" Then she swayed as if about to faint and I caught her to me, afraid she might slide under the rail of the bridge, and when I looked at the water again the dreadful body was gone. Not moving downstream but simply gone, as if it had never been.

We did not tell our grandparents, or our parents. We never spoke again, even to each other, of what we had seen by the bridge. I spent the remaining week of our holiday in miserable anxiety, wondering if I *should* tell someone - in case it was a sign of a great calamity to come and one that might be stopped or escaped from. The spa was now well protected from avalanches, but might there be an epidemic or a war? Then I thought, if there was, we could do nothing to avert it, and silence was best.

There was no such catastrophic event. The curse, the omen, whatever it was, fell only on poor Trudy. Grandmother might have said it was a vision sent by God to punish Trudy for her levity about the dead. Grandfather would no doubt have said something else. Trudy was never the same again. There were no more requests for stories, no more forbidden expeditions. She became increasingly withdrawn, eccentric and uncontrolled and when she was twenty she was sectioned and has never left the clinic where she still is now. I visit her once in a while, and she regales me with the doings of her imaginary friends, now realer to her than I am, especially a pretty dark-haired girl who wears harem trousers and red slippers with long curled toes.

## Peripheral Vision

In the *trompe l'oeil* room were fruits and flowers that seemed real enough to pick, objects that looked like real objects on real shelves standing against the museum wall, portraits with gowns that flowed out of painted frames as if the frames and the silks and velvets were solid enough to touch. Portraits of faces that changed, like moving shutters, when you passed them. And one portrait that changed not to a different face but a skull.

"This is a momento mori," explained the courier. "In the Middle Ages there were many pictures like this, especially after the plague. There were the 'Dance of Death' paintings you can see in churches, and the grotesque effigies of half-decayed corpses you find on certain tombs. The idea is to remind you that you must die and urge you to lead a virtuous life and prepare to meet your maker."

"I think it's cool," said a teenage boy, walking past it again to catch the effect.

"I think it's revolting," said a fat woman at Philli's elbow.

"But who would want to be painted like that?" asked a man behind them.

"Oh, lots of people," answered the courier. "It was fashionable to be morbid. Some even kept their own coffins in the house and practised lying in them. One famous poet slept regularly in his coffin."

"He can't have had much of a sex life," the teenager said.

Philli Loris only glanced at the skull, shuddered and passed on. This exhibition was not her cup of tea. Ingenious, yes, but not what she thought real art. Art with a soul. Rembrandt, El Greco, Turner ... though one had to admit the technique was amazing.

Phillipa Loris had become Philli after her divorce. Her absconding husband (that was how she thought of his adultery) had always called her Pip. Becoming Philli was to mark a new start in life, though the name was a bit young and trendy for fifty-seven and a bit like all those Jennys turned to Jennas, Susans to Susynns, Debbies to Debras. But she felt it was right, just as it was right, early redundant and comfortably off, to throw herself into new activities, volunteer work, evening courses, cultural travels like this museum tour. Next time she'd be more adventurous... Eastern Europe or West USA ...

"Dreaming, are you?" said the man who had spoken earlier. "They're all moving on to the next room."

"Oh," said Philli, annoyed, for this was the kind of thing her ex-husband used to say. Dreaming, are you? She hurried to catch up and passed the skull again, meeting its bony blank expression in a corner of her eye.

A few days later, when Philli was home and shopping to restock her fridge, came what she was to think of as 'the first one'.

She was at the check-out counter and just stuffing her groceries into her environment-friendly bag-for-life. The pretty young cashier sported an interesting hairstyle, a shoulder-length bob parted in the middle with strands combed to alternate sides. I wonder if I could do that, thought Philli. No. Too young. What am I thinking of? She looked again at the cashier and dropped the bag she was holding, for what she saw was not a face but a skull. A skull with hair still on it, strands neatly combed to alternate sides, the hair absurd and incongruous above the blank black noseholes and eyeholes filled with that terrible darkness, a skull with moving jaws, a gibbering skull because the girl was speaking.

"Is something wrong, Madam?" asked the skull.

"No, no. I'm just a bit clumsy today," Philli answered quickly. The vision had only lasted half a minute. The girl's face, thank God, was back.

Maybe I'm doing too much, thought Philli, maybe I should slow down. Cut out the extra half day at Oxfam, get more sleep, remember what Dr Linkbein said, divorce is a trauma ... A good glass of wine when I get home and think no more about this.

She did think about it and read for a long time that night before turning her light off and trying to sleep. When she finally slept, there were no dreams. There never were to be any dreams of skulls throughout her whole ordeal. But the second incident was the very next day. Robby Headly, her cheerful plumber, looking up from putting in a new sink drain, suddenly turned to Philli not his smiling face but a grinning skull with a metal piece in its jawbone from an injury repaired many years before.

When the plumber left, Philli called her best friend Anna, whom she'd known since university days. It had to be a phone call only; she could not risk visiting Anna and seeing her face, in the midst of their talk, turn into a skull.

She had forgotten that Anna, another divorcee and living alone like herself, was passionately wedded to the internet. Anna said at once, "You know what I'd do first thing? I'd go online."

"Online? But how? But why?"

"Look up the symptoms. Seeing skulls or whatever. See if they fit any known eye or ... other disease. And if that doesn't work put it on your Facebook page –"

"I'm not on Facebook."

"Okay then. Some other social network. Or set up your own website and ask for responses. I'm sure you're not the only person something weird like this has happened to."

"I really don't think I want to do that."

"If you're worried about doing it I'll do it for you and see what I can find out." Anna sounded delighted at the prospect.

"If you want," said Philli. "Meanwhile what I will do first thing is see my GP."

Then she went out to get another Rioja and passed a neighbour whose cheery "Morning" emerged from a hatted and sunglassed skull.

Three times?" said Dr. Mackintosh. "But you say it hasn't happened now for a week. It might well not recur. I'll give you a mild anti-depressant –"

"I am not depressed. Except at the thought of this happening again."

"Or sleeping pills, if you're not sleeping well –"

"I had all that stuff after my divorce. I end up sleeping till noon and being miserable all day."

"Fine, I'll just give you the prescriptions and you get them if you want. Meanwhile, see an optician. Your eyes should be checked regularly anyway at your age. Oh – by the way – you're not seeing my skull are you?"

"I would tell you at once if I did."

"Good. Well, consult the optician and come back if your – strange eyesight goes on."

Philli walked out, feeling better, then turned back into the reception room, having forgotten her scarf, and saw a skull in a polo-necked sweater poring over the computer at the reception desk.

The optician was sympathetic and deeply interested. "It started with a picture? Tell me, have you ever had migraines?"

"A few times, when I was very young. Not for decades."

"Ah. There's something called an optical migraine. It can come after looking at something very bright, like a small TV screen in a dark room. You get coloured zigzag patterns in front of your eyes. I wonder if the lighting on the picture you saw could have triggered something like that."

"I don't see zigzags. I see skulls, and not just any skull. I see the actual skull of the person. No two are alike, just as no two faces are. It's as if I suddenly have x-ray eyes."

"And always just the skull?"

"Yes, thank God. Like in the picture. If it were also the bones I think I'd go mad." She stopped, realising what she had said. The optician quickly put in, "Well, we needn't worry about anything like that. Macular degeneration can do strange things – though I've found no sign of it. Still, I'll check you again in a couple of weeks, just to be sure, and we mustn't, I fear, rule out the brain. Your GP should send you for a CAT-scan."

Later that day Anna phoned, very excited.

"I haven't found anything in Wikipedia or the medical sites, but I've set up a new email account for you and a website and asked for people with similar experiences to email you."

"You've done *what*?"

"Oh, don't worry. Nobody will know it has anything to do with you. A lot of creepy Goths and religious freaks have sent replies. And one DIY suicide site wants a link. I've deleted them all except for four. So have a look at your new email. It's *benignbony@worldwit.com* and the password is deadhead59."

"I'll do it later. I've got enough on my plate right now. I'm going to the neurologist tomorrow and have a CAT-scan and all the works."

"Do they think that's really necessary? Right away?"

"Yes. And so do I. It's happening more and more. Now it's about two a day. I meet everyone in dread, waiting for it to happen. As much as I can I keep my eyes down. People must think I'm a foot fetishist, I look so much at their feet."

"My God, poor Philli." Anna for once was at a loss for more words, then "Well, let me know at once what they find out, and if you need anything, I'm there. But whatever, I think it might help to read what those others have to say."

The scan and the tests, like the optical examination, showed nothing wrong. Perfect health, said the consultant. "I think the next step is –" Philli knew what the next step was, and wondered (as the consultant had twice changed shape while talking to her) if she would now have to spend long sessions addressing a skull.

"So it hasn't happened with me yet?" the psychiatrist asked.

"No, not yet. It doesn't happen with everyone. Or all the time. By the way, do I have to talk to a whole panel – to your colleagues listening behind the glass? Is this to assess me for certification?"

"No, not at all. We are a team. We see all our patients first as a panel."

"So you don't, at this point, classify me as insane?"

"Mrs Loris – Philli – no one has mentioned certification. You are functioning normally. You are fully cognisant that what you see is not real. That is very hopeful. Besides," he added in what Philli thought must be his ultra-soothing voice, "we no longer lock people away unless they present a real danger to others. Or to themselves. In-patient treatment these days is nearly always voluntary."

"I'm glad to hear that," said Philli. "But I might even be willing to enter a clinic if it's the only way to help. I really can't go on like this." Her voice broke. She had determined in vain to be calm. She really didn't trust this man, but by now she was willing to try anything. Either cure, or Dignitas, she thought, but better no mention of that; then they *would* lock me up. And that would be the worst of all, in a padded cell with skulls coming in to attend to me. Skulls from whom I cannot escape. Wonder what Dignitas would say. A case I bet they never had. Dear Dignitas, I want to die because everywhere I see Death. This made her, in spite of everything, smile.

Dr Toper jotted down a note. Easily abstracted, definitely bipolar. His colleagues in their eyrie were writing, on their laptops, much the same. "Now then, Mrs Loris. I'm sure we can do something to help you. As I said, you are still cognisant of the unreality of what you see –"

"You don't understand," Philli said. "I do not hallucinate some kind of Freudian symbol. I do not hallucinate. What I see *is* real. I see through the face to the skull."

Yes, yes, thought the psychiatrist, delusions of grandeur, the x-ray eyes of Superman. Why only skulls, he wondered. It might be a subject for a case study if they found out. "And now suppose you tell us more about how this all began."

In despair, Philli accepted the treatment, the useless sessions with Dr Toper and his colleagues listening from behind the window, the prescriptions they wrote. She imagined skulls wagging together, discussing, comparing notes.

Nothing stopped the skulls appearing. But the drugs allayed her anxiety. She no longer contemplated suicide.

At least, not immediately. She slept a great deal, and was often tired and groggy when awake. She gave up her new activities, and watched a lot of mindless TV. On the screen, as in mirrors, there were no skulls.

She read the emails Anna had not deleted; there were of course many more since, most of which Anna again deleted at once. "Too upsetting. Totally wacky. Really, people's disturbed minds…"

"I'm a disturbed mind, remember? Anyway it was your idea."

'Dear benign bony, here you are and what a gift from the gods. I thought I was the only one. I have been seeing skulls ever since I dropped out of medical school after my first dissection class. Usually they're floating in the air like balloons. Sometimes they get bigger like someone is blowing the balloons up. Then sometimes they burst and there's like a flash of lightning behind my eyes. Do you think I should see someone about this?'

Philli answered, 'Yes, see your doctor, and I don't think we should correspond any more.'

Delete.

'Dear Benign Bony, There is a group that can help you. We are people who see beyond the outer surface, beyond the everyday. In the midst of political crises, climate change, terrorism and wars, we have maintained our clarity of vision. What you are seeing is THE TRUTH – that is the failure of our politicians and our institutions can lead only to the victory of DEATH. And why? What lies behind all the failures? It's not Davos, it's not the big corporations and the big banks, it is another organisation, an organisation so secret and so powerful that we dare not name it here, but if you join us, you can find out. We have PROOF and WITNESSES prepared, when the time comes, to testify at the risk of their lives …'

Delete.

'Dear Benign Bony, There is a medical device that will clear your dreadful visions. No injections, no pills are involved. You must simply wear, without removing it for a week, our bracelet of wooden beads from the rare Melmothisan tree, impregnated with the rare oils of a flower that grows only on...'

Delete.

(Obviously Anna thinks I am ready to try anything which in fact I am).

But not this.

'Hi benignbony, this is crossbone Charlie answering your call for help. I have had visions very much like yours. As you're an intelligent woman – my guess is you are a woman – I want to know a whole lot more about your visions. Who are the different people whose boneheads you see (no pun intended – but maybe it's symbolic, the whole thing I mean. Maybe the people you know are just not interesting enough. Maybe they're dead inside. Ha ha). Maybe you need a new focus in life. Why don't we meet and put our heads (no pun intended) our heads and our deadheads together?'

What on earth was Anna thinking of, to keep this one?

Delete.


Anna, so busy with the website she had created she scarcely had time for anything else, finally agreed to remove it. But meanwhile other websites had formed on the subject. The internet buzzed with Gothic visions, tales of headhunters, *memento moris* to view or buy. Philli went off the internet altogether and spent longer hours in front of the TV


Her son rang, not his usual monthly call from San Francisco where he had lived for the past seven years.

They were not close; Andy had been more his father's boy. "Mum? I'm worried about you. You sounded so strange last time I called, so I emailed Anna to see if you were okay and she said you've been having some kind of weird – sightings or something? Mum, can you tell me what's wrong? Should I come home for a visit?"

"No!" Philli answered, so sharply her own voice startled her. "No. Anna shouldn't have told you anything. My eyes were doing funny things. Some kind of optical migraine. I'm getting better but it takes time. No, don't even think of coming." The thought of seeing Andy's skull was unbearable, even in her tranquilised state. "I'll try to get over and visit *you* next year." She went on chatting as brightly as she could. Andy felt relieved, if just a bit hurt by the vehemence with which she had refused his offer. She had a new life, she'd told him; he might just be in the way. After all, he'd never been as close to her as he was to his dad.

Philli felt herself getting more sluggish, more indifferent. She began to have headaches, occasional dizzy spells, and sometimes her speech slurred and there were pins and needles in her hands. At first she'd been too relieved by the calming effect of the drugs to really research possible side effects. Now she did and was appalled. She asked for a different prescription but it seemed the NHS had nothing else applicable. She asked the psychiatrist to reduce the dose, and "isn't there any kind of talking therapy that might help?"

Not with this advanced psychosis, thought the psychiatrist, and sighed. He was a great believer in modern medication. "Well," he said after some thought, "my colleague Millmoss does cognitive therapy. We could have a go at that. But I must warn you not to expect miracles."

"My x-ray eyes are already something of a miracle,

wouldn't you say?"

"You do not really have x-ray eyes, Philli. You have a fleeting vision whose cause we can't yet understand."

"It's not a vision. I see the real skull. Warts and all. I mean cracks and all. I've checked. I've asked people. About old injuries, teeth … the skulls are real."

That's what they all say, thought the weary doctor. "Well, come in on Tuesday and we'll see what Millmoss can do."

Philli came in on Tuesday and was ushered into another office where a smiling chubby man awaited her. On his desk sat a large human skull.

"Does this skull frighten you?" asked Dr Millmoss eagerly as soon as the preliminaries were over, and Philli had explained her problem.

"No," said Philli, already impatient. "What frightens me is seeing the skull inside living people's heads."

"I want you to pick up the skull and handle it."

"Okay, fine, though I don't see what this has to do with what I've told you. I don't see how handling a dead person's skull is going to change it."

"Please, Mrs Loris, just do as I say."

Resignedly, Philli picked up the skull.

"Now, please, I want you to put it down, but look into its eyes, and stroke its head. I mean, the top of the skull."

"I can't look into its eyes because it doesn't have any. Look, I've picked it up as you said. Why do I have to go on touching it?"

"There you are. You see, you have an aversion to this skull."

"Most people do have aversions to skulls. Skulls mean death. Surely an aversion to skulls is natural."

"That is true. But death happens to all of us, Mrs Loris, sooner or later. It is your obsession with death that we must try to deal with. Obsession is often a sign of two conflicting emotions, both attraction and repulsion. But I will not burden you with theory. Just pick up the skull once more. . Thank you, that's it. You can hand it back to me. You see, I hold it perfectly calmly. Have you ever done any drawing, Mrs. Loris? Any art classes?"

"No. I don't think I have any talent in that line."

"Talent doesn't matter, Mrs Loris. I think one thing that might help is if you were to attend a class in anatomical drawing. And later on I would suggest we make a list of some other things you could do. Maybe even volunteering in a hospice ..."

Philli was gazing at Dr Millmoss, and suddenly said, "There's a metal plate in your right cheekbone. It must have been badly shattered once. A triumph of modern surgery, wouldn't you say? Would *you* like to tell *me* about the accident?"

Dr Millmoss dropped the skull, which, as his floor was carpeted, fortunately did not break. He bent clumsily to pick it up; when he straightened again his face was red and his hands were shaky.

Philli could not repress a smile.

"I have discussed your case with Dr Millmoss," said Dr Toper at Philli's next appointment. "He doesn't think intensive cognitive adversarial aversion therapy is the right one for you."

"I'm not surprised," said Philli.

"However," went on Dr Toper, "He suggests an appointment with a colleague who has quite a different approach, a mild, non-confrontational one, which seems beneficial for many patients where other therapies fail. It's called patient-centred affirmative therapy. Are you willing to try it?"

"You know, Dr Toper, that I'm willing to try anything."

"Now, tell me about your concerns," said Dr Feralder, whose skull was mercifully invisible. Philli did, finishing with, "I don't just see any skull. I see the real skull of the person I am looking at."

"You see the real skull of the person."

"Yes. No two skulls are exactly alike. So it's not a hallucination. It's as if I had x-ray eyes."

"You feel as if your vision goes straight through to the bone."

"And of course this happening – it's happening more and more – besides being very frightening – has really restricted my life."

"It was bound to curtail your activities and to restrict your life."

"Exactly. I now wear very dark glasses most of the time and sometimes I'd like to go out with an eyeshade and pretend to be blind."

"You would like to block your vision so what so upsets you doesn't happen."

"I was just beginning a new life after my divorce and now everything is in ruins."

"You feel that your seeing of skulls has demolished your new life."

What is this person, Philli was beginning to think, a doctor or a parrot? But she finished the session and went back for three more. Dr Feralder's echo technique was curiously soothing and what was more soothing still was that his thin serious face stayed solidly on his head.

Other skulls, however, continued to multiply.

Philli tried hypnosis, Philli had a session of REBT, a session of MDT, a session of QRND. The hypnosis didn't work; the others, she could sense at once from their approach, would be as useless as the previous therapies had been.

Should she try psychoanalysis? At least she'd have the shrink sitting behind her and could avoid seeing his skull. No, that was too long a process. Despairing again, as with the reduced drug does her physical state was better but the terror at what she might see had come back, she began once more to collect material from Dignitas and Exit DiY International. A trip to Mexico to get the requisite fast drug? Mexico, the country of skulls, where they passed out skulls made of sugar at festivals … no. But then … skulls, death festivals, religion … she remembered something she had said to Dr Toper. My vision is already a miracle.

Why not turn to the church?

Philli was not a churchgoer. She had been confirmed and vaguely believing as a young girl, but the belief had waned and she had scarcely attended church since. Still, since her ghastly visions were inspired by memento moris, something from the age of piety, perhaps a bastion of piety should be turned to.

Though reluctant to confide in yet another person, she consulted her one seriously Anglican friend. Hetty was all sympathy and eagerness to help. "Father Groves, my vicar, is really a wise and wonderful man. I'm sure talking to him is worth your while. "

Father Groves' church was very high church, lots of candles, statues of saints, a smell which could only be incense unless Father Groves wore a very strong and rather oriental-smelling brand of aftershave. He listened quietly to Philli's story, then he asked, "Do you ever pray, my dear?"

"Not really. Unless just saying please God make this damned – sorry, make this thing go away counts as a prayer."

"When we say please God, it is always a prayer." Father Groves sighed, "Yours is a very unusual case. You say medicine and psychiatry have not been able to help you, and that is why you have come to me. But have you thought that your visions may be a path to God, a tortuous path but one that God has chosen for you?"

"No, Father Groves. I have not considered that. I am not even much of a believer." No longer overwhelmed by her drugs Philli was becoming almost daily more cynical, more ironic, more assertive, as if the sight of people's skulls gave her authority and often even carte blanche to be rude. Not everyone is blessed with x-ray eyes. "What is that old saw? If God is God he is not good, if God is good he is not God. If my heavenly father sees this as a way of bringing me back to the fold he certainly got me – my – back up before I get there. If you can forgive the clumsy pun."

"Teilhard de Chardin," said Father Groves wearily, referring to the quote. "Although in the end he *was* a believer. However - would you perhaps agree to see someone else? An old friend of mine, Brother Aloysius, in the Bartholomine monastery at Otterpie. I know, it's a long way to travel."

"But the Bartholomines are Catholic. Aren't you rivals?"

"Rivals? Not really. It has long been my personal hope that the schism would end. In any case, if you don't mind, I will tell him about you. He is a (wise and wonderful, thought Philli, even before he said it, oh good, now I see inside minds as well) wise and wonderful man who has dealt with many extraordinary problems and has changed many lives, including lives of those who came to him without sharing his belief, or mine. I think he may be able to help you. Do go and see him."

The Bartholomine monastery was on a small island off the Irish coast. The monastery offered retreats to both men and women, at fairly high prices; Bartholomines were a declining order but their reputation remained unblemished and high. The seventeen monks prayed a good deal and ran an organic farm. When Philli checked in for a week, as Father Groves had recommended, she was already feeling better. There had been only two skulls on the ferry. One was very upsetting, as it was a child's; Philli usually managed to avoid looking at children.

The island was bleak but beautiful. Waves crashed against its low but dramatic cliffs. Seabirds swooped and called, herring gulls, great black-backs, kittiwakes. The monks' vegetable plots, meticulously tended, were so rich in colour and variety they might have been planted for ornament only. The low monastery building with its row of wooden doors and simple chapel seemed organic too, as if grown from the island. Best of all, the monks who received Philli kept their faces.

Philli's first appointment with the illustrious Brother Aloysius, whose name was spoken in reverent tones by the other brethren, was not until the next morning. She was shown to her cell, a little white-washed room with a sparkling white bed and a chair and table of beeswaxed ash. Only the simple black cross above the bed relieved the whiteness. Philli went for a walk, breathing in the salty air, watching the birds and the late sunlight on the tossing water, and felt better still. After a simple meal of bean soup and bread and goat cheese was brought to her cell, she went to bed at once, and fell into a deep refreshing sleep.

Father Aloysius was a stocky little man in a billowing brown habit, who reminded Philli of benevolent Dickens characters in old book illustrations. He really did seem to radiate calm and peace. He heard Philli's story to the end and did not speak for a long time.

Philli waited, praying (if it were a prayer) that his face would stay.

"Many are called, but few are chosen," Brother Aloysius said at last.

"I don't think I understand."

"My dear, I know you are not of our faith. But you have no doubt heard of Bernadette Soubirous. You have no doubt heard of Lourdes." He had a strange, slightly foreign accent which Philli could not place.

"Are you suggesting I go to Lourdes? Do you think that would cure me?"

"No. I do not think you require a cure. I think this vision, now so horrible to you, is a call from God."

"I still don't understand. I want to get rid of these skulls. They're making my life total hell. I hoped you could help me."

"It is God who can help you. It is not given to those who are chosen to have only beatific visions. Bernadette saw a beautiful lady. You see skulls."

But where is the healing spring, thought Philli with her now habitual cynicism. "So – what do you think the skulls mean? What does God want me to do?"

"That will become clear when you have accepted Him. Your suffering now, like the dreadful tumour that killed poor Bernadette, is a sign of His Grace. God has given you a mission, a mission to inspire or perhaps to lead. Yes, perhaps to found a new order. God is purifying you. We must now wait for His word. Your skulls are a sign that you can see beyond the surface of things, that you can see through what other people see. God's patience with us is infinite. We must learn to be patient with God."

"But I don't even believe in God any more."

"Perhaps that is why you are seeing skulls," said Brother Aloysius, "not like Bernadette seeing the beautiful lady His holy mother. You see beyond life to death but you do not yet see beyond death to eternal life. When your faith returns I think the vision will change. Why not give God a chance."

The new Bernadette, thought Philli wryly. But I said I was ready to try anything. And I haven't seen a skull since I got off the boat.

"I'll think about it," she said. And then, as she got up and started for the door, she saw the bland face of little brother Aloysius change to a skull, an especially vivid and shiny skull, which remained even when she looked it full in the eye sockets, even when he rose to say his goodbyes; which remained longer before her eyes than any skull ever had.

Maybe this God, after all, has given me a sign, thought Philli. There were no more sightings, but she left the island the very next day.

"You say you're willing to try everything," said Anna. "Talk to my neighbour Moira. She seems to have a gift of healing. And I know of some people she has really, really helped."

"I suppose you've already told her about me. How many people have you told? For God's sake, I've already had a reporter from some weird magazine turn up on my doorstep yesterday. And Dr. Toper is just as bad. He wants to discuss my symptoms with a whole group of students in London. I'm going to be downright famous if this goes on."

"I haven't indentified you, don't worry. Moira is a bit flaky but really nice and she'd love to try to help."

Moira and her two friends – like the shrinks, they seem to be teams now, thought Philli – were all middle-aged, and very intense. Moira had bushy, fluffy hair and wore a kaftan. Sidonie had long plaits going grey and lots of bracelets and rings. Louisa had green nails and a pentacle tattooed above her cleavage and her mannishly short-cut hair was the colour of baby carrots.

The witch's coven, Philli thought, but she didn't see their skulls. So that was a good beginning.

They listened avidly to Philli's story. They said nothing about delusions or hallucinations. They talked heatedly to each other about chakras and channelling, terms new to Philli, but she felt more empathy from them than anyone who had heard her out before. At last Moira said, "Your Father Aloysius was right in a way. You are being sent a message and we have to find out what it is. And from where and from whom. Suppose we start with the Ouija board?"

The palette on the Ouija board moved quickly and without hesitation. It spelled ONEX. Then it paused. Then it said BADPLANT, and paused again. After that it said FURAT and SUVIR.

After SUVIR it refused to move.

Furat Suvir, Moira said, sounds like the name of an Arab terrorist. And BAD PLANT – the only recognisable words – were possibly a warning that this Furat Suvir was going to plant a bomb somewhere.

Moira got very excited about this and said she thought she should tell Special Branch what the Ouija board had said.

Sidonie, the calmest of the three, pointed out they had already once reported what might have been a warning of terrorist attack and had been laughed at, and anyhow they were supposed to be searching for an explanation of Philli's vision of skulls.

"But this could be an explanation," Moira insisted. "Furat Suvir is going to kill all those people. That's why Philli sees their skulls. And isn't Xenos the Greek word for stranger? So an alien terrorist is going to kill a lot of people. That's what the message is."

The others disagreed. The argument went on and on. Philli listened patiently, now seeing two of the faces turning to skulls after all. She decided not to tell them. Finally Moira turned to her. "What do you think, Philli? Does that interpretation sound right?"

"No. Maybe. I don't know. If you want to report it, go ahead, but I think you'll be laughed at, like that other person was."

Louisa suggest they try the Ouija board again to see if now it would move.

The Ouija board said LANDERVA and then determinedly stopped again.

"Landerva! That's the name of the organic moisturiser I use," exclaimed Sidonie. "Which is an anagram for Lavender."

"So maybe a bomb or a radioactive poison will be hidden in a bunch of lavender? Or could it be, Sidonie, that you were thinking of buying more of that cream? You told me the other day you were out of it. So your thoughts could have been interfering with whatever presence was here."

The argument was still percolating when Philli left.

Philli walked along the street to her bus stop; driving had been out of the question since the fear of seeing an oncoming car with a skull in it. Dignitas, she wondered, or a bigger dose of Philamelodon, Dr Toper's latest recommendation. I don't even feel capable of making that decision. Dear God, how tired I am. Then she became aware of a wheedling voice at her elbow. "Will you buy some lace off the gypsy, lady? Will you buy my lucky lace?" Philli turned to see a small woman with a nondescript face topped by thin dyed blonde hair. Her pink T-shirt, red skirt and scuffed trainers had obviously seen better days, and the way she held out her thin strip of garish maraschino-coloured lace looked as if she hadn't had much luck herself.

"No, thank you," said Philli automatically – and then stopped. "I don't want lace but I want – Do you tell fortunes? Do you look into crystal balls – palms – anything like that?"

"Your fortune, Madam? If you will cross the gypsy's palm with silver –"

"I don't really want my fortune told. I want to ask you something. Maybe you can help me."

The gypsy stood waiting, smiling her professional beggar's smile, while Philli dropped coins into her hand, and then listened to Philli's story. As she listened, her smile went, and a strange disturbed expression came over her face. At the end, she asked, "Are you seeing my skull, Madam?"

"No. I'm not seeing yours at all."

The gypsy drew a deep breath and then exhaled, as if with relief. "Now I tell you what you must do. You go back to that place – yes? The picture where you first see a skull. You must walk past the picture again – but other way, so you see first the skull, then the face. Then you run from that place and you never never go near it again."

"Oh thank you," said Philli, "thank you." She reached into her purse for more money, but the gypsy did not wait. To Philli's surprise, she gave back the coins Philli had given her, and hurried away as if afraid of some contagion. But Philli did not puzzle over this long. She was too eager to rush off and make reservations for travel to the town with the *trompe l'oeil* exhibition and try the gypsy's cure.

The cure worked like a dream. Within a few weeks Philli gave up her therapist and her drugs and spent the money she'd saved for Dignitas. She returned happily to a normal life.

The gypsy, meanwhile, with no word to anyone else, moved with her two daughters back to a small village in the Carpathian mountains which was her ancestral home.

Three years later, even earlier than climate scientists had predicted, the sea level rose fifteen feet.

And the last great pandemic began.

## Lycanthrope House

Author's Note:

I saw the name 'Lycanthrope House' on a real house in Penzance just before I left for a long trip abroad. By the time I returned and got up the courage to knock on the door, as my characters did, the name was gone and I could not remember which of the several terraced houses it had been. So the mystery of the name, and its disappearance, remain unsolved.

In the seaside resort where they stopped for groceries, parking lots were crowded and the charges high. Dilly would have opted for any space they could get. She was tired and it was late; the shops would soon be closing. Rob, however, insisted on driving around until they found a space on a side street. It was a street of identical Edwardian terraced houses. They were not big or imposing but they all had names in gold-colour italic letters on the glass panel above the door. Saffron Villa. Galleon Gables. Glynis House. Lycanthrope House. When they came back from the nearest grocery and were putting their supplies in the car, Rob said suddenly, "Wow. I don't believe it. Look at this name."

Dilly sighed. Rob, the American she had rashly joined on a camping trip in Cornwall, was fascinated by the quaintness and eccentricity of English houses, English towns, English customs, English names. Rob went on staring at the gold letters. "I wonder if the people who live there now named it. I wonder if they even know what it means."

"What does it mean?" Dilly said without interest. "Anyway, we'd better get going."

"Ly-can-thro-pee. Or lycanthrope? I've never heard anyone *say* it. It means werewolf. I've got a mind to just knock on the door and see who does live there."

"Bloody hell, Rob. We don't have time. Anyway, those names were probably put there a hundred years ago when the houses were built. Those old letters."

"Italic letters," said Rob.

"You know everything, don't you?" Ly-can-thro-pee. Eye-ta-lic. So why d'you want to knock on the door?"

"I said. To see who lives there. And find out how the house got its name."

"I don't see why you should give a fuck about all that. We were going to the Lizard today. We'll never find a camping place before dark."

"You're a Goth," said Rob resentfully. "You of all people should be curious."

"It's probably just some stupid weird joke," said Dilly.

"So what's being a Goth then?" Rob looked down at Dilly who was as petite and slim as he was tall and bulky. Her hair was half carrot, half inky black and spiky, and although it was summer she was wearing high black boots and tights, a black mini and a black sweater. She had a nosestud and a lipstud as well as almost black lipstick and black nails, the usual multiple earrings and probably piercings in other places Rob had not yet seen. Getting to those other places had been, for Rob, one of the purposes of their camping trip. Despite all the stupid gear she was a very pretty girl.

Dilly, for her part, thought Rob sophisticated and interesting. He was eight years older, he'd been around. Also, she liked the customized van he'd done himself with an English friend. She had told her mother she was going on the camping trip with a couple of girlfriends, who would cover for her. She had also lied to Rob, telling him she was twenty when she was not quite seventeen. She suspected he might have guessed though. Maybe he thinks he's getting a virgin, Dilly had said to her friend Jane and they'd both burst out laughing, though Dilly in fact had only been shagged three times and not liked it much – but that was not the kind of thing you would admit.

So far, the trip was not going well. They'd left London early and Rob had wanted to stop at a lay-by and shag her. Dilly said no, it was too soon, she'd spent ages making up (she enjoyed the appraising eyes at petrol stations and coffee shops) and she just didn't feel like it yet, not at that hour of the morning. Which in fact she didn't, and besides she didn't want to seem too easy. So Rob, frustrated, was increasingly impatient and patronizing, talking to her like she had no brains. All the more reason to make him wait. Only now she was tired and wanted to get off the road and start on the vodka he'd bought them.

"Being a Goth is not a joke. It's a style. It suits me. I like black," Dilly began indignantly.

Rob interrupted. "There's a bell. I'm going to ring." Before she could make another protest, he did.

There was no answer. "See," said Dilly, "there's nobody in. Please let's just go."

"Maybe the bell doesn't work. Let's try the knocker." The knocker was a big one of polished brass and seemed very loud on the quiet street.

"Oh shit, Rob. Maybe they don't want to be bothered." But this time there was a sound of footsteps and then someone opened the door.

"Yes? Sorry, we don't buy anything," said the man in the doorway. His beer belly was so big it protruded through the doorway and Rob stepped back. He was wearing a bathrobe whose two sides just managed to meet over the belly, tied with a cord that did not match. There were felt slippers on his feet and under the bathrobe, blue pyjamas. Like his shoulders, like his stomach, his face was broad and sagging. The face was so covered with stubble the features were almost masked. He was either growing an untidy beard or had not bothered to shave for days. Nor had he combed the wispy grey hair that suck out in tufts around his big head.

"Oh, I'm sorry," said Rob at once, thinking this person must be someone either sleeping off a huge hangover or sick in bed. "I'm sorry to bother you. We were just fascinated by the name of your house. We couldn't help trying to see if it was you – whoever lives here – named it and why - "

We, thought Dilly. Damn you Rob. I never gave a shit.

"So you know what it means." The stubbly face relaxed into a smile. "Come in. Do come in. We're always so pleased if strangers take an interest. Literacy is rare nowadays. Most young people don't know what anything means. But don't get me started on our cultural decline. But come in, come in, and I'll tell you all about it."

Dilly hesitated and was about to speak; but Rob took her hand and pulled her after him into the house.

"Now," the man went on, "What can I get you? Can I make you some tea? But no – it's already past six. Best hour of the day. Time for drinky-poos. What would you like? Gin and slimline tonic okay? Or whisky? Wine?"

Drinky-poos, thought Dilly. Sodding hell. Still, if she had to put up with this, drinky-poos was a good idea. "White wine," she said, with no 'please', and Rob said, "I'm driving, so just a small whisky with soda and ice, please."

When they were seated in the small lounge, a very ordinary room with a three-piece suite, a couple of Staffordshire spaniels on the mantelpiece, seascapes on the walls, and a pea-green fitted cord carpet that vaguely co-ordinated with the patterned upholstery of the suite, their host went into the kitchen to do the drinks. He was rather a long time.

"You should have said something simple like beer. How long is this going to take?" Dilly, seething with impatience, tapped the heel of her boot against the base of the couch.

"Will you stop bitching? We'll go right after one drink."

Their host reappeared then, bearing a tray with coasters, glasses and expensive looking bottles. "Whisky and soda for you, sir, white wine for the lady."

"It's Rob and Dilly," said Rob.

"So pleased to meet you, Rob and Dilly. I am Richard Fainton. And welcome to Lycanthrope House." Formally he shook hands with them both. His hand felt podgy and moist; they both withdrew quickly from the handshake. This produced something like a faint smirk and eyebrow raise on the stubbly face. So he noticed, thought Dilly. So good on him. I just want my drink and get out of here.

"You must excuse my attire," Richard Fainton began. "My partner is a terrible night-owl and not very well. Heart, you know. And we are both insomniacs. So we do sometimes get up rather late in the day, and poor Randy often doesn't make it downstairs at all, I have to bring his trays up to him – but never mind our troubles. Now, as to Lycanthrope House. I didn't name the house. I came here just as you did. I saw the name, I knew what it meant, and fascinated by it I knocked on the door. I got into a long conversation with the man who owned the house and who *had* named it. And that conversation has continued for twenty years."

"I don't get you," said Rob.

"Well, wasn't it Cyril Connolly who said, marriage is a continuing conversation? Oh sorry, I forget. The young don't read Cyril Connolly. Randy – my friend who owns the house – of course we both own it now – became my partner. We have been together ever since."

"Wow," said Rob.

Old faggots, thought Dilly.

"So I guess for you it was a lucky name," said Rob. "But why did your friend name the house like he did?"

"I think – he was much younger, then – he wanted to scandalise the neighbours. Also, Randy is passionate about folklore. When he was at university he wrote a thesis on Eastern European legends which was later published by Oxford University Press. I might add, to much academic acclaim."

"Have other people knocked on your door?"

"Not very often. Not many strangers come down this street. You, I guess, were just looking for a place to park? Yes, I thought so. And then, I think people who know what the name means may be afraid to knock. You wouldn't believe how superstitious and credulous people still are. I have seen an occasional one look at the name and then hurry on by. Randy gets a chuckle out of it."

"I bet he does," said Rob.

Richard turned to Dilly. "Perhaps you get some of the same reaction sometimes to your garb. Many would consider it eccentric. I find it very becoming."

"Thanks," said Dilly curtly, wondering what garb meant but certainly not going to ask.

"It's a shame Randy's not down yet. He could tell you so much. He began his research with the French legends of the *loup-garou* – the man who at night changes into a wolf – but he found that in other cultures the possessed take other forms, usually that of the most powerful animal around. Though not always. The *loup-garou* can sometimes be a hare – in some cultures even a tree – but always it feeds on living flesh or practises evil witchcraft on human beings, and if it is wounded it goes back into human shape and retains that wound on its human body... Sorry, I'm rambling on. Folklore was not what I read at university but Randy's enthusiasm is infectious. Would you like a top-up?"

"I think we should go," said Dilly. "And Rob shouldn't have any more, he's driving."

"I think I can effing decide how much to drink," said Rob. "Sorry," he added, turning to their host.

"Top-ups for both then," said Richard smoothly. "Don't worry about the expletives, please. I am quite used to that from Randy. In fact the two of us get quite foul-mouthed when we start ranting about how philistine society is becoming. The idea of knowledge for its own sake has gone out the window. Thank goodness we are both retired and no longer have to cope with the modern world."

"So you're retired," said Rob. "What did you do before?"

Don't get him started on something else, thought Dilly as Richard refilled their glasses. We'll never get out of here.

"Oh, this and that. Randy did a bit of teaching and I used to restore paintings. Lots of art around here and a damp climate. You'd be surprised how much work I had. Randy still writes a lot about folklore. Tends to write all night and sleep in the day. He has just finished an article on an interesting local legend – but I mustn't start again. Cheers. Or as we used to say, bottoms up." Dilly, on whom the first drink was having an effect, suddenly thought what a funny thing for a gay to say and giggled. Then to cover that – she thought she caught Richard giving her what her granny would have called an old-fashioned look – said quickly, "Cheers."

"D'you think I could use your loo?" asked Dilly a few minutes later.

"Yes, of course. It's upstairs. I'll show you."

On their way to the end of the upstairs hall they passed two doors, one closed, one slightly ajar. Through that one came a faint wheezing sound and a waft of musty unpleasant smell. "Randy's asthmatic," whispered Richard. "Heart, you know. Sometimes he stays up here all day because he can't do the stairs and the only loo is up here. We keep meaning to have a downstairs toilet put in but we haven't the money."

"That's rough," Dilly said politely, thinking they certainly had money for expensive booze and wondering if Randy was too sick to wash very much. Thank God they wouldn't have to meet him. "Couldn't you get a grant for it? My granny did."

"No, no," said Richard. "I have thought of it, but Randy wants nothing to do with the Council."

When Dilly got back downstairs, Richard was spouting on again, and Rob, having quickly downed his second whisky, looked bewildered and sleepy. Dilly picked up her glass, gulped the rest of her wine and said, "Thanks so much, Richard, but we really have to go. We'll be late for a camping place on the Lizard if we don't go right now. Rob? Are you coming?"

"Okay, okay," mumbled Rob and somewhat laboriously got himself up.

"Look," said Richard awkwardly, stammering a little, "I'm a-fraid I'm guilty of having kept you rather long. Why don't you stay the night? I can rustle up some food. I have to cook for Randy anyway eggs or something, and you can sleep in the van, or the house if you like – and get off early in the morning."

"Well," said Rob, "that's really nice of you – but –"

"*No*," said Dilly. "We've got to go."

"I'm not sure I'm fit to drive," said Rob. "That second whisky has really got to me."

"Why don't you have something to eat and then

decide? It was quite a lot of alcohol for an empty stomach. Sorry, my fault. I should have had some nibbles on offer but we don't keep any, I'm afraid. We don't get much company these days, and Randy has a terrible nut allergy. One peanut or cashew and poor Randy could be gone –"

"Thanks, but no thanks. We have food in the van. The van hasn't got a fridge, we have to eat the stuff today," Dilly said, determinedly making for the door.

Rob followed. "Hang on, Dilly. I'll go get the food. We can have it here. Sorry, I really don't think I should drive now."

"I could drive," said Dilly.

"Are you bonkers? You told me you don't even have a licence yet. Besides, you too have been drinking, remember? Sit down and chill out, why don't you?"

"I'm coming out with you," Dilly said.

"I'll see what we have in the fridge," Richard put in, heading for the kitchen, as if sensing that Dilly was hostile, and uncomfortable alone with him. Dilly wavered, then settled back in her chair. Richard and Rob returned simultaneously a couple of minutes later, Rob with the sandwiches and strawberry yogurts they had left in the van.

Rob was fuming. "Shit, I don't believe this. Some effing dickhead has let all the air out of two of my tyres. And I've only got one effing spare."

"Oh dear, oh dear, oh dear. Oh not again." Their host sounded painfully upset. "It happens all the time, I'm afraid, though not too much on this street. Vandals, idiot kids. Any out of the county car they'll vandalise. Terribly chauvinistic, the locals here."

"Well, I guess we have to stay." Rob resignedly sat down again, putting the food on the table with the bottles.

"Let me take your food to the kitchen and put it in

the fridge," said Richard soothingly. "Then it will be all fresh for you tomorrow. I'm sure we have enough for us all for tonight. Oh dear, oh dear. Poor Dilly does look a misery." He studied here with his small sunken eyes, then added suddenly, "I have an idea. I have something to cheer you both up. Something to calm the nerves before we start supper." He turned to Rob and said, more softly, "I have some really good Moroccan. Do you think Dilly would like that?"

"Dilly?"

"Rob, I just want to go. We're supposed to be – alone together on this trip. We can find a café. And then sleep in the van," Dilly said, almost tearfully but more weakly.

"Let me talk to her a minute," said Rob. Richard discreetly went to the kitchen again. Dilly, feeling strangely tired, pulled herself together and began angrily, "What makes you think we should smoke with this guy? Suppose he's an undercover cop? Suppose he grasses on us? He could be anything. I don't like it and I don't like him. We can still go. We can call the AA –"

"I haven't paid them yet. And – Richard a cop? Don't be a complete nitwit. It's his house, it's his risk. He's just trying to make up for what's happened. He's just being nice. He's a bit of a weirdo but he's okay."

Richard, returning, spoke as if he had overheard. "I'll get my own garage to look after you in the morning. Now then. Just a wee puffy wuffy before we have some eats." He began, not very expertly, to roll a joint. "Oh dearie dear, the old paws have got cramped. Those years of doing restoration – all that fiddly work – afflicts the aging fingers. Some days, you know, worse than others –" His speech was becoming slightly disjointed as if he like them was affected by the drink.

"Let me do it," said Rob, ignoring Dilly's warning glance. Suppose he's a cop, she thought. Suppose this whole sodding thing with the name on the door is a trick to get kids like us to come in and smoke. I wouldn't put it past the drug squad to plan something like that. Only the other day she'd been on a train and they'd gone through with their sniffer dogs – shit, what was the matter with her? She'd almost said that out loud.

"Dilly?" Rob was repeating her name and passing her the spliff and in spite of her resolutions she took a deep drag on it. And then another, and another. Almost immediately she felt better.

All was silent for a while. Then there was loud coughing upstairs and a querulous voice called out, "Dickie? I did ask you not to smoke in the house."

"Okay, we'll go into the garden," Richard called back, but neither he nor the young people made a move. After another minute, Richard carefully put out the joint. There was another silence. Then the querulous voice called out again. "Dickie? Have you finished? Should I come down now?"

"Yes. But remember your digoxin. I'm not going up the stairs to fetch your digoxin again."

"I have all my pills, Dickie, in the pocket of my robe."

"Make sure you do," said Richard sternly. "You don't remember much these days." Then as an afterthought he added, "Dear old thing."

"I'll be careful on the stairs, Dickie."

"Yes, old thing, I hope you will. So come on down."

# Prester John

I first heard of the patient John Q through a paper published by the late Dr Alphonse Wunderkind, in the *Autism Therapy Journal*, Vol. XIV, No. 3.

John Q was admitted to Dr Wunderkind's clinic a few months before the paper was written. He was thirty years old, but his poor physical condition and unkempt appearance made him seem much older. He was brought by a sister some twenty years his senior, who had looked after him since his parents' death. The parents were poor Portuguese immigrants who had spent their lives in menial jobs and with great difficulty brought up seven children: six girls and a desperately longed for son, the youngest, John.

John had apparently never learned to speak, and though he seemed to understand a little of what was said to him, was so withdrawn and erratic in his behaviour that he was diagnosed early as autistic. As a baby, he was markedly unresponsive; as a child, he spent most of his time sitting in the kitchen staring at the wall. Sometimes he sang to himself in a low deep hum. "It sounded like church music," the sister commented, "but it wasn't like no music on the radio or nothing or the songs my mother sang." Occasionally John would get up and do a strange stately dance, shuffling three steps forward, three steps back, while slowly nodding his head or holding out his palms as if making an offering. He usually ate what was put in front of him, and with some difficulty was toilet trained by the age of eight. Everything he did was in the same slow, deliberate, and stately fashion. On the whole he was gentle and tractable. He simply remained closed off in his private world.

Far from rejecting their seemingly hopeless child, his parents showered him with attention and love. Deeply religious and very naïve, they were convinced that John's strange behaviour had some mystical significance and that one day there would be a miraculous cure or a miraculous revelation to explain why he was as he was. Knowing the cruelty of the streets where they lived, they kept John inside and away from prying eyes. The new child was sickly, they explained to neighbours, and under doctor's orders to be left indoors. There was one session with a therapist, which seemed to make John worse. He began to wet his bed again and did not move from his corner for several weeks unless bodily lifted. After that his parents refused all treatment, and the over-burdened social services left them alone.

The parents were adamant that John should never be institutionalised. They extracted a promise from their children that John would be looked after as long as any of them lived. This job in the end was left to Maria, the eldest sister. One daughter had gone back to Portugal, one died in a car accident, one, Maria said bitterly, became a call girl; the other two had families of their own and didn't want to know. She herself was living with a younger man who kept urging her to get rid of John, but she felt bound by her promise. And she might have gone on taking care of him if he had not suddenly begun to talk.

It began from one day to the next. John simply opened his mouth and spoke, loudly and at length. What he said seemed addressed to no one; he maintained his fixed stare at the opposite wall. Maria could not understand what he said. There were a few words she recognised, many she did not. It made no sense to her at all. Still, she was delighted he was no longer dumb. She thought that at least John was coming out of his inner world.

Sadly, she was wrong. Nothing changed. For weeks John did not speak again. Then one day she came home to find he had escaped and was standing on a corner of their street, haranguing the passersby. She grabbed John and led him away. One well-dressed man called after her, "your friend is giving a speech right out of the Middle Ages." She didn't know what he meant. She thought perhaps he meant John sounded older than his years.

From then on John erupted into speech "like a volcano" every few days or weeks, and made determined efforts to get outside again. He always spoke in the same flat but booming voice, "like a politician or something". It happened any time of the day or night, and sometimes went on for almost an hour. The neighbours began to complain, and Maria's boyfriend said "it was either John or him, John had to go."

Maria felt terrible because of the promise to her parents. But not only did she fear to lose her boyfriend; she depended on his income. All she could do now was piece-work at home, as she no longer dared to leave John alone. Besides, John's sudden declamations were so unnerving she herself was often unable to sleep, wondering when he would "start shouting about peacocks and diamonds and stuff", or walk to the door and rattle it, trying to escape. Maria said she was "under awful stress, ready for a nervous breakdown, scared of losing even the little work I've got left". When her parents had exacted their promise, John had been silent and obedient. No one could be expected to cope with this new John. Besides, said Maria, "he scares me now. He's so different. I don't know what he'll do next." She heard about Dr Wunderkind's clinic on a TV programme about autism and went to see him. She didn't have any money, but thought maybe Dr Wunderkind would be interested in taking John as a patient "because of that very weird stuff he talks". To convince Dr Wunderkind, as it might be weeks before another outbreak, she taped part of one of John's speeches and took it along.

This tape – and the two others Wunderkind later made himself, and quoted in his paper – was so extraordinary that I determined to see John for myself. Not only was so unusual a patient well worth a look, but he seemed a perfect case for a trial of tridoperosthotin, the new drug I myself had been working with and which had only just been released for clinical trials.

Wunderkind's little clinic survived on private patients and an occasional grant. Wunderkind had undergone several vicissitudes. He had begun, he said, as a disciple of Bettelheim, though he had never met the celebrated doctor, but soon switched his allegiance from Freud to Jung and retrained as a Jungian. Now, he said as he led me down a shabby hallway to the day-room, he was becoming "entirely eclectic. I am developing my own theories also. In this connection – in any connection – John is a most fascinating patient. But you will see for yourself."

Seven listless men sat in the frayed chairs of the day-room. A male nurse was channel-hopping with the TV remote. "Stop that please, George," said Dr Wunderkind sharply. "You know it upsets them."

"In a minute," answered George, and went on.

Dr Wunderkind reddened. "Now, please," he said. George turned the TV to a children's puppet show and left it, whistling faintly between his teeth and tapping the remote control on his knee. Dr Wunderkind did not appear to have a very dedicated staff.

If the patients had been upset, they did not show it. None of them were watching the TV. One was laying out cards, another clasping and unclasping his hands, a third staring fixedly at an untied shoelace. They were very quiet and very much in their own worlds. The most striking was a gaunt man with a beard and fierce staring eyes. He sat rigidly upright with his hands on his knees, as if posing for a formal photograph a century ago. Dr Wunderkind nodded in his direction, but I would have guessed anyhow that this was John. And as if on command for my visit, John began to speak.

"Should you desire to learn the greatness and excellency of our Exaltedness and of the land subject to our sceptre, then hear and believe. We, the Lord of Lords, surpass all under heaven in virtue, in riches, and in power. Seventy-two kings pay us tribute. In the three Indies our Magnificence rules, and our land extends beyond India, where rests the body of the holy Apostle Thomas. It reaches towards the sunrise over the wastes, and it trends towards deserted Babylon near the tower of Babel.

Our land is the home of elephants, dromedaries, camels, crocodiles, metacolinarum, cammetenus, tensvetes, wild asses – ("You're a wild ass yourself," muttered George the nurse, not too softly for me to hear) – white and red lions, white bears, white merles, crickets, griffins, tigers, llamas, hyenas, wild horses, wild oxen, and wild men, men with horns, one-eyed men with eyes before and behind, centaurs, fauns, satyrs, pygmies, forty-ell high giants, Cyclopses, and similar women; it is the home, too, of the phoenix and of nearly all living animals. We have some people subject to us who feed on the flesh of men and of prematurely born animals and who never fear death. When any of these people die, their friends and relations eat him ravenously, for they regard it as a man's duty to eat human flesh. Their names are Gog and Magog, Anis, Agit, Azenach, Fommeperi, Befare, Conei-Semante, Agrimandi, Ventefolei, Casbei, Alanei.

These and similar nations were shut in behind lofty mountains by Alexander the Great, towards the North. We lead them at our pleasure against our foes, and neither man nor beast is left undevoured, if our Majesty gives the requisite permissions. And when all our foes are eaten, then we return with our hosts home again."

Though John continued to stare straight ahead during his long speech and his booming voice never varied in its strange robotic cadence, the other patients were riveted. They ceased their own activities and sat to attention like schoolchildren, gazing raptly at John until his recital was finished.

It had been like that from the beginning, Dr Wunderkind said. The other patients ignored John, as he ignored them; but when he spoke they listened like children hearing a fairy-tale, and since his first speech even the worst of his fellows had treated John with consideration and deference.

"George, however, hates him," said Dr Wunderkind. "I do not know why. This is George's problem. I have long wanted to fire George, but it is hard to get anyone better to work in this place at a salary we can afford now. And George at least does not drink or take drugs on the job; he does not, to my knowledge, ever abuse them, he does not let them run away. But he has taken a particular dislike to John. Well, we will have to see how things turn out."

John's speech was certainly extraordinary, and I wondered if someone had taught him this bizarre text. Could the sister have coached John to recite to get him off her hands – or had he learned to read in some unobserved way? Had even Dr Wunderkind himself, perhaps, knowing that such a patient would get him much attention, especially in Jungian circles... but that idea I dismissed at once. Wunderkind had never given anyone cause to doubt his honesty. Besides, the difficulty of such teaching and the risk of being found out were too great.

It is true that autistic patients often manifest extraordinary gifts. There are mathematical and musical idiot savants; there was the son of antique dealers who knew every style of period furniture in minute detail, the little girl whose drawings recalled the art of Marino Marini and were even more powerful. But even if John had learned to read, where would he have obtained so esoteric a text? It was of course possible that it had featured in some TV or radio programme, that it had struck a chord in John's disordered mind and he had memorised it on the spot. Possible, but unlikely in the extreme, and if John had such a memory that in itself would make him a marvel.

I asked Dr Wunderkind if I myself might study John, and if it would distress John if I conducted a few tests. Dr Wunderkind was delighted by my interest. "Do what you like, my dear colleague. You could stick pins in him and he probably wouldn't notice." I also asked to see John's medical records and any other material Dr Wunderkind had.

My research confirmed that John had never attended school, and a visit to his sister confirmed that the family was barely literate. "We never had no books in the house," the sister said. "Just the Bible. My mother had the Bible in Portuguese."

I looked around her dingy apartment with its yellowed net curtains and Disney figurines. No, it was not the sort of home in which you would expect to find books. Her companion, sprawled in front of the TV, kept his back to me. "Can you turn that down, honey?" asked the sister timidly. "I think this gennulmun want to ask me some more questions." The man turned the TV off abruptly and went out, banging the door.

I was reminded of George, the hostile nurse at Wunderkind's clinic. "At least he doesn't abuse them," Dr Wunderkind had said wistfully. I noticed fresh bruises on the sister's leg; she caught my eye and pulled down her skirt. Poor John, I thought, was well out of it.

My research led nowhere; and unlike Dr Wunderkind, who claimed to be developing a theory that would explain the mystery of John, I myself had none. However, I remained fascinated, not least by the deference and calm his recitations imposed upon his fellow patients, as if indeed they were awed by the presence of a great Lord. Meanwhile, John's speeches grew longer and more elaborate; and rarely did he repeat one.

"All riches, such as are upon the world, our Magnificence possesses in superabundance. With us no one lies, for he who speaks a lie is thenceforth regarded as dead; he is no more thought of, or honoured by us. No vice is tolerated by us. Every year we undertake a pilgrimage, with retinue of war, to the body of the holy prophet Daniel, which is near the desolated site of Babylon. In our realm fishes are caught, the blood of which dyes purple. The Amazons and the Brahmins are subject to us. The palace in which our Supereminency resides is built after the pattern of the castle built by the Apostle Thomas for the Indian king Gundoforus. Ceilings, joists, and architrave are of Sethym wood, the roof of ebony, which can never catch fire. Over the gable of the palace are the two golden apples, in each of which are two carbuncles, so the gold may shine by day, and the carbuncles by night. The greater gates of the palace are of sardius, with the horn of the horned snake inwrought, so that none can bring poison within.

The other portals are of ebony. The windows of crystal, the tables of gold and amethyst. The columns supporting the tables are amethyst and ivory. The court in which we watch jousting is floored with onyx in order to increase the courage of the combatants. In the palace at night nothing is burned for light but wicks supplied with balsam. Before our palace stands a mirror, the ascent to which consists of five and twenty steps of porphyry and serpentine. We look therein and behold all that is taking place in every province and region subject to our sceptre. We look therein and behold all that is taking place at the four corners of the world.

In my kingdom there are ants which eat men, but by night they mine gold for my coffers, and however much I may choose to spend my coffers are never emptied. In my lands there are men who live only on heavenly manna, and by magic and incantation they tame the flying dragons and ride them though the air to do my bidding. I have five precious stones that can make the air hot or cold according to my will within five leagues of wherever I shall place them. I have other stones which can turn water to milk or wine, others which will cause fish or wild game to assemble for slaughter, still others which, if sprinkled with dragons' blood, will cause a fire great enough, if I choose not to quench it by my incantations, to consume a quarter of the earth."

Wunderkind and I did our best to track down the strange words and names in John's recitations. Some, like the mythical names Gog and Magog, were already known to us. *Anis* was possibly Agnis, the Hindu God of fire. *Sardius* was a gemstone mentioned in ancient texts. But what was Sethym wood – and what strange creatures were "metacolinarum, cemetennus, tensevetes"? Where had John found these clearly Latin names? I decided to consult the prominent historian Dr Harris Ender, sending him the tapes Wunderkind and I had made of John's outbursts. There was an instant response; Ender phoned me, breathless with excitement.

"Your patient," said Dr Ender, "is repeating the contents of a strange Medieval document, the Epistle of Prester John. There are different versions, most of them last published about a hundred years ago. Your patient seems to have gleaned material from several different versions. This is quite amazing, considering your statement that he cannot read and has never, as far as you know, been in contact with anyone scholarly. The document is not easy to track down. One would need access to a good library, probably with old books."

"But who was Prester John?" I interrupted, quite breathless myself.

"Prester John was a legendary figure who probably never existed. Some reports said he was descended from the Magi, but historians now think the legend was based on a twelfth century Nestorian priest-king of the Orient who supposedly wrote a letter to the Byzantine emperor Manuel. The letter was almost certainly a forgery. It was not published until 1500, and new marvels were added to it, inspired by the legend or by travellers' tales. The Epistle describes a king of incredible glory, power, and wealth. If the letter were genuine, its writer himself might have been psychotic; even a king of the credulous Middle Ages could not, unless he were mad, have claimed to posses all the magical treasures and powers the letter describes. Do you think Dr Wunderkind would let me see his patient?"

I said I was certain he would, but my heart sank. I had been hoping to persuade Wunderkind to try shock treatment, followed with a dose of tridoperosthotin. Wunderkind did not appear to be treating the patient at all, and surely John deserved some effort to make him better. The elaborate speeches he had learned – for he must have learned them, heaven knew how – indicated a prodigious ability to memorise, and a sometime contact with the outside world. And only if his state improved could we investigate the secrets of that memory. But Wunderkind's Jungian bias might make him see John as some kind of mystical reincarnation and make him unwilling to try any treatment which might cut off John's bizarre monologues.

Once again I wondered about my colleague. As a Jungian he would be versed in mythology, might even have known about the Epistle. Could it after all be Wunderkind himself who had secretly taught John to spout his marvels? But no, I had the testimony of the sister. "Peacocks and stuff." Then how and where had John memorised the Epistle?

I was now even more anxious to try the tridoperosthotin, hailed as a truth drug as well as therapy, a method of uncovering buried traumas. Dr Raymond Crankwell, according to his recent paper, had had much success with a patient similar to John. But John was Wunderkind's patient and I needed his permission.

Meanwhile John was adding prophecy to his list of wonders.

"In my mirrors, the steps to which are twenty-five steps of serpentine and porphyry, I have beheld a flood like unto the great flood of old, and also I have beheld a great fire, and I have beheld mountains of ice sinking under the waters and I have beheld how a hundred thousand forests shall fall and shrivel under the sun. The nations of Gog and Magog, Anis, Azenach, Agrimandi, shall burst forth as it was foretold, for the end of the world is nearer and the anti-Christ who has claws upon his feet and who can speak with all the tongues of men shall walk again upon the earth."

"It's this Millennium," said George to me sourly. "They're just as bad, some you see out on the streets. I just hope the doctor don't bring in anything worse."

George, Dr Ender, Dr Wunderkind himself – someone may have talked a little too much about the interesting case of Prester John. Before the historian could visit, before I had even broached the subject of treatment, John disappeared.

It was Dr Wunderkind who phoned me, in great distress. It seemed a priest had appeared at the clinic, saying he was from John's sister's church and she had asked him to visit John as she herself was sick and could not come. The priest was soft-spoken and polite. He asked if he might take John for a little walk in the garden. It was a mild sunny day, and as Dr Wunderkind just then was interviewing another patient, George took it on himself to assent. "I didn't see no harm in letting the old guy out in the sun." Coaxed by the priest, John seemed willing to follow him. When after half an hour George went to get John in for his cup of tea, John and the priest were nowhere to be found.

Wunderkind called the police, who paid minimal attention. The city was full of lunatics who appeared, disappeared, re-appeared, and disappeared for good. The police did put out a Missing Persons bulletin and questioned John's sister. She knew nothing of the mysterious priest, nor did the church she attended.

John's face with its blank staring eyes, prominent bones, and wild wispy beard was striking enough to remember, and some weeks later a witness came forward. She had seen a man she thought must be John at a religious meeting she was taken to by a friend. The meeting was run by a strange little sect who called themselves the Pentecostal Lights. "Sounds like a frigging cigarette," said George when Dr Wunderkind told him, but the news made him visibly uncomfortable. As well it might, since it was he who had let John go out with the mysterious priest.

That a crank sect should kidnap John, no doubt to present him as a holy incarnation, made perfect sense. The police did follow up the report, but without haste. They had more important things to do, we were made to understand, than search for an old lunatic whom no one except his doctors wanted to find. By the time they checked, the Pentecostal Lights had dissolved into darkness. The rooms they last rented were deserted, the last rent unpaid. The witness's friend swore she had never attended but the one meeting, and that only "because somebody said those people could cure my arthuritis." Both women also swore they knew no one else at the meeting, and wouldn't even recognise anyone there whom they chanced to see again; they only remembered John because of his extraordinary appearance. As he had not spoken at the meeting and no one had referred to him, we could not even be sure it was John they had seen. If the women were lying, if they had been warned off by the Pentecostal Lights, there was no sign of it. Dr Wunderkind hired a private detective for a short period, all he could afford, but the results were no better than those of the indifferent police.

John's wild face remained on display a little longer. Wunderkind put up posters privately as well, and I agreed to give my office telephone number as a contact so Wunderkind's clinic would not fall into more disrepute. I had several phone calls, some clearly mischief-makers or other disturbed individuals, a few that hinted at genuine leads. Once an excited man telephoned, "Hurry, hurry, Mister. There's a wild guy with a beard, and he's talking about salamanders, worms that live in a fire, and he's got quite a crowd. I think he's the guy in your picture."

"I'll come right away," I said. "Where are you?"

"It's the corner of – the corner of –" He seemed

suddenly confused. "I just ran to the nearest phone. I guess it's 20th and South. You got to hurry, the crowd's beginning to go."

When I reached the corner in question, fighting my way through rush hour traffic, there was no sign of a crowd or of John, and no one I buttonholed on the street had seen John or heard the speech. I went back to the corner several times but it was futile; sadly as the report of "worms that live in fire" made me think John might really have been there.

Dr Wunderkind was determined not to give up. He spent hours and days following every clue. He neglected his patients, and ignored colleagues who warned him that he would soon bankrupt his clinic and make himself ill. Unfortunately for Wunderkind, tantalising leads continued to emerge. The next was a police report concerning a vagrant in Pontive City, two hundred miles away. The vagrant, arrested for shoplifting, told a strange story. Among the tramps who gathered at a nightly fire under a bridge, drinking beer and heating cans of soup, was a man the others called Preston John. "He talked a lot of crap about sitting with twenty bishops and stuff like that. Where would this guy know twenty bishops? He didn't have a cent to his name. The funny thing was how the other guys listened to him. They're a rough lot, but nobody would hurt John. A guy with a beard, he was, and funny eyes. He coughed something awful. Coughed and coughed and skinny as a rail. I think if you want to see him alive you ain't got much time."

After this description, which again led nowhere, we were not surprised that the next reported sighting was in a T.B. ward – in Baldrockie, another hundred miles on. He was described as a frail old man who muttered so strangely one nurse recorded some of what he said.

He claimed to own a "a fountain from Mount Olympus, not three days' journey from Paradise", and that could he only drink of it he "would remain forever only thirty years old." By the time we reached Baldrockie, the dying man had somehow dragged himself out of bed while the night nurse was busy elsewhere and vanished into the dark streets. Though still wearing a hospital gown and so even more conspicuous, he was never seen again. The hospital authorities were even more upset than Dr Wunderkind; this patient, not expected to survive, had a particularly virulent and contagious strain of T.B.

By this time our posters and investigations were establishing a new urban legend. The media took up the story and soon there were sightings of 'Prester John' all over the country. Now that his speeches had been identified and publicly quoted, there were bound to be many hoaxes, as well as call from fellow psychotics. We soon despaired of sifting out any genuine leads. Reports continued to circulate, and poor Wunderkind was haunted to the end of his days by a few psychic research societies who thought John was indeed a reincarnation of a great mythical king and that they could establish contact with him through their mediums, ouija boards, or whatever they specialised in.

I suspect that Dr Wunderkind himself entertained a similar theory, and that the loss of his most precious patient was one from which he could not recover. The clinic soon went into liquidation, and shortly after that Dr Wunderkind himself, broken and prematurely old, died of pneumonia following a heart attack.

It was some five years later that the garden of the clinic was dug up for new construction and a body was found.

George Headley, the nurse, was tracked down and

questioned, none too kindly, by the police. He confessed that the body was John's. "I couldn't stand that guy going on any more about his gold and rubies and all that shit." He himself had unlocked the gate and pushed John out into the garden, hoping he would run away. The story of the mysterious priest was one he had concocted as his alibi. Since the only witnesses who could have seen the priest were autistic, he did not feel he would be con-tradicted. When a few days later John came wandering back at night and clamoured at the gate, George, again alone on duty, had hit him with a spade. Only, George said, to make him run away again. "But John wouldn't go. He just kept talking. Louder and louder. I couldn't stand that stuff." In the end he hit John hard enough to kill him.

George was given a life sentence. The case, however, did not end there. Some strange forensic evidence came to light. There were conflicting medical reports about the DNA and the age of the body in the garden. It was as if John's identity proved elusive even in laboratories. George died in prison before there could be a re-trial, and the question was dropped. At all events, no other possible identification for the corpse in the garden was ever found.

So the conclusion of the case of Prester John remains as mysterious as his life or the myth of his forbear. The urban legend continues. There are still reports of a wild bearded man talking glorious nonsense; but more and more nonsense seems to focus on prophecies of doom, in keeping I suppose with ecological crisis and the hysteria that accompanied a millennium. A new Prester John letter, with many embellishments, even circulates on the internet.

I greatly regret that a course of tridoperosthotin,

which might have solved the enigma of John and also cured him, can never be tried; the drug has now been withdrawn because of its possible side effects. A patient with the symptoms of John is a very rare gift.

# Dispension Island

Tracy Troutman is texting her best friend Sally Demold.

Tracy is bewildered. More than that. Bewitched, bothered and bewildered, as an old pop song had it. "Why me?" she keeps asking Sally. "Why me. I don't understand."

What Tracy doesn't understand is why she, as one of many girls employed by her boss, Conrad Gray, has been chosen to accompany him as his 'kind of p.a.' at a gathering of top business people and government officials on Dispension Island, a private island they own, where no outsiders are even permitted to land.

Her computer skills are not exactly first-rank. She is a little forgetful. She is easily flustered. She has an irritating nervous giggle. She is a lot less educated and sophisticated than most of the girls employed by Mr. Gray and his partners. It is part of their image to have girls around who look competent as well as chic, who impress the traders, even though there's not that much for the girls to do. Women's Lib never did get far with eliminating that image thing. She wonders if Mr. Gray is hot for her. The thought sends shivers down her spine. Mr. Gray has never singled her out, has never had her in his office alone, has never even shaken her hand, let alone hugged her. Not that she would object. In these difficult times, girls forgive others for not being too Me-too. And Mr Gray is really very attractive. In fact Mr. Gray is a dream.

Not everyone, of course, would consider Mr. Gray a dream. His face is pleasant, his legs are slim, and his hands, thinks Tracy, are beautiful. She does like beautiful hands in a man. However, he is the wrong side of fifty. His hair is receding, and he has a very definite paunch which his good suits – yes, even in these days of rationing and the New Austerity, there are still good suits, maybe because once again there are private tailors – his good suits cannot hide.

In fact he is shaped rather like a pear.

Tracy wouldn't mind. She is shaped much like an apple herself. In these days of rationing and veganism shapes like hers and Mr. Gray's are increasingly few. Maybe it is a bond between them. Maybe Mr. Gray feels more comfortable standing next to a girl who is not a stick-figure. But she hardly has time to puzzle over the Why Me question because Mr. Gray has told her they are to leave for the Dispension Island conference the very next week.

Tracy has come a long way for the child of a single parent, brought up on the wrong side of the high-speed railway, a child whose education stopped after a single year of business college. She's working for an important corporation. They don't call themselves corporations any more. After the climate catastrophe, when government controls and rationing came in, a lot of corporations were supposed to be broken up and a lot of government out-sourcing was re-sourced back in. But corporations have ways of re-forming themselves. Somehow the same people turn up, with lower salaries and lower profiles, but still there, with the same connections, maybe as part of the new Government itself. Not all of course. Some are still in prison. But then, even those once high-profile ex-prisoners often land on their feet when they get out. As Buffy Molmeth, the girl at the next desk, who is senior to Tracy and gets to deal with Classified Material, likes to say mysteriously, a lot goes on behind the scenes.

Mr. Gray's corporation makes robots for border defence. The robots are efficient and sensitive, but must be accompanied by sniffer dogs. No one quite knows why but it is the law. It has been quite a job pairing up robots and sniffer dogs but Tracy's firm has found the secret which is why the business is such a success and although businesses now are to keep to their remit and not invest in unconnected firms, Security Robotics has tentative tentacles in other directions. As Buffy Molmeth says again, a lot goes on behind the scenes.

Tracy, after endless texts to her best friend Sally asking advice, spends her last clothing coupon on a lemon-yellow pinafore shorts suit made from recycled tofu wrappers, which is on sale and so not returnable, and then decides, after a long consultation with her full-length mirror, that it looks like shit.

In the end she arranges a hurried meeting with Sally and swaps the lemon-yellow shorts suit for a powder-blue off-shoulder top and while roll-up shorts lined with a print of extinct bluebells made from whatever. She buys artificial nails to match, made from recycled computer screens and has her hair tinted blonder with a dye made from recycled house paint. After all this, and trying to get her office work up to date, there is only just time to pack, and to read with dismay a text from Mr. Gray. "Do not worry what to wear. Bring minimum clothes. On the island we all dress in artificial artisan grass garments provided by the management."

They reach the island in Mr. Gray's private aeroplane. There is no more public aviation to speak of; anyway, with the weather so erratic and so many previous holiday resorts ruined by drought, flood, fire or revolution, there are not many places worth flying to. But the executives of very successful enterprises still have private planes and enough carbon coupons to fly them once or twice a year.

There are three other executives on the plane with Tracy and Mr. Gray, two of indeterminate gender and another man. They give Tracy a perfunctory greeting; then the four go into a deep hushed conversation, ignoring her. Tracy is nervous and uncomfortable. The shorts are too tight and even the off-shoulder blouse is too hot; the plane's air-conditioning doesn't seem to work very well. From time to time, Mr. Gray glances at her and once leans across the aisle to her single seat and gives her arm a long affectionate squeeze. "Are you alright, Tracy?" he asks. Tracy gasps and nods, too thrilled and embarrassed to speak; but Mr. Gray has already turned back to his companions.

After what seems like an endless flight, they have a bumpy landing on an empty airstrip which seems to have been hacked from the side of a hill. Mr. Gray turns again to Tracy. "We had to have this little airport made," he explains. "The former airport is now under the sea." Bicycle rickshaws pulled by scrawny men in shorts come to collect the five. Mr. Gray, looking at Tracy's puzzled frown, feels obliged to explain again. "We have no chargers here, so no electric vehicles. But distances are small so we can use the good old-fashioned form of transport that was used here years ago."

"I suppose it's lucky it's not a big island," Tracy says.

"It's lucky it's there at all. It was once a small country. This is what's left of it."

"So – what do people eat here? I mean, how do they live?"

"There aren't many inhabitants. We have supplies brought in and they grow a few plants on their side of the hill. Mostly, they work for us, when we're here. They think themselves fortunate." Mr. Gray smiles and squeezes her arm again. "It doesn't look very exciting from here, I know, but you'll see something pretty when we get round the hill."

And that is about as much as they can talk with the bumping of the rickshaw on the stony track.

A mile or so on, Tracy does see something pretty. A little settlement of tidy thatched huts with a few palm trees and beds of brilliant tropical flowers. A beach of yellow sand, a blue, white-bordered, kidney-shaped swimming pool, a central palm-trunk pavilion which is obviously for meetings and parties. It looks like the tourist brochures Tracy found among her mother's papers after she died, places her mother might have hoped to go to when she herself was very young. Before the big CC.

As far as Tracy knows, she never went.

Tracy moves to take a picture. "No photography here," says Mr. Gray quite sharply. Tracy, blushing, lowers her phone. "And I'm afraid no messaging either," he continues in a more gentle voice. "You can send a text from the machine in our office," he indicates a hut "- once or twice a week if you want. Your phone probably won't work on the island anyway. Why not let me have it to put in our safe and I'll give it to you before we leave again? There aren't many places to keep your things, as no one needs money or gadgets here, and more than one person has lost a phone in the sand. The sand shifts a lot if the weather turns nasty."

This seems a bit strange to Tracy but obligingly she gives Mr. Gray her phone, at which he smiles and does another squeeze; this time on a bared shoulder.

Mr. Gray walks Tracy to her private hut, which has a table, two chairs, and a grass skirt hanging on one of them. "You can keep your own tops or - bras," says Mr. Gray with a hesitation Tracy thinks becomingly discreet. Then he asks, "Hammock or cot? The cots are very comfortable but some guests prefer the hammocks. The huts are quite private at night; we have woven screens you can slide across the doors. Anyway, no one trespasses here. There's a communal shower and several loos, those little huts, do you see?" He gestures to the right. "No en suite here, I'm afraid. But then that's what we all come here for, to live simply, exchange ideas, and build up team spirit."

Tracy giggles. "Oh cot, please. I've never even laid in a hammock before. It must be bad for your posture, don't you think?" What she is in fact thinking is, how could you have sex in a hammock? That is, if Mr. Gray did plan to visit her at night, a hammock might be a problem.

Mr. Gray just says, "Cot it is then," and calls to one of those skinny servants – why are they all so skinny? – to bring the cot, which has quite a luxurious looking mattress with it but which is extremely narrow, almost too narrow for Tracy herself.

The next ten days do not exactly go by in a whirl. The most exciting thing is the food, mostly brought to Tracy in her own hut. It is abundant and as good as could be. Everything that could be invented to dress up soya, tofu and a few farmed insects is done. Tracy is too young to remember animal meat-eating days, though her mother had sometimes served intensively farmed barnacles for a special occasion. Tracy eats her fill, sleeps like a log, and takes a dip in the pool every morning and every afternoon. Usually she has the pool to herself. Mr. Gray advises her not to swim too energetically and not to do any walking; it was dangerous in the heat. There is anyhow nowhere to walk to. Tracy does stroll around the artificial grass and palm-leaf village, but Mr. Gray discourages this too. "We have to keep huts open to get the sea breeze; no electricity, so the breeze is our air-conditioning, and people value their privacy. We had a commercial spy who got in here two years ago and since then, though I'm sure it couldn't happen again, some guests are nervous."

Mr. Gray occasionally calls her into his hut to transcribe, on his ancient portable typewriter, some notes for the motivational talks he would be giving in the course of the year. "What an antique!" Tracy exclaims when she sees it. "It must be a really expensive collector's item."

"It is," says Mr. Gray with pride. "So be careful with it." Tracy promises she will be.

Mr. Gray's speeches are immensely repetitive and boring, all about keeping up the old spirit of free enterprise in the midst of regulation and austerity and not much left for enterprise to work on but surely the days of Friedman and even Ayn Rand would come back and the barrenness of the planet would be ultimately rectified by technology and ...

Tracy wondered who these speeches were meant to address and why, when she has been brought here as a p.a., there was so little for her to do; and why that was as much as she saw of Mr. Gray. For the first seven nights, though unable to figure out how it would work on the cot – maybe it would be the rush flooring instead? – she put on her best 'sheer, like pale green sea-foam' so the internet had described it, recycled plastic nightie, in hopes of Mr. Gray's visit. After that the nightgown goes to the laundry hut presided over by another haggard servant and Tracy, tired from the heat and phlegmatic from the well-fed lassitude of her days, falls every night at once dreamlessly asleep.

All in all, the dream journey with the dream Mr. Gray is not what Tracy had envisioned. Her weekly text to Sally, sent under Mr. Gray's rather eagle eye, soon reduces to "More perfect weather," and "Wonderful meal last night," while praying Sally would not be indiscreet enough to ask what else she was up to – about which she need not have worried, as, Mr. Gray explained, no answers could be received "except in emergencies. We really try here to exclude the outside world. That's why our conferences are always a success."

When did they actually meet, and about what did they confer? Mostly Tracy followed Mr. Gray's advice, but when she has finished the two chick-lit books and out of date fashion magazines Mr. Gray provided, all about how to stretch your coupons and make more out of less, she does venture more around the grass huts again. She passes a bigger hut at the edge of the village and cannot resist peering inside, where there is an array of masks and fancy dress costumes, the masks rather grotesque, like African stuff from museums. A servant appears and in a language she can't understand says something angry and waves her away.

On another stroll she hears a voice, which is not Mr. Gray's, intoning the same phrases: "In these hard times it is easy to lose sight of the old free spirit and blame ourselves for just being human, for thinking it was our libertarian free-market values that led to the exhaustion of the planet, and not the greedy demands of the ignorant envious multitude ... and now nature itself has reduced the multitude to manageable proportions by that great waste-swallower the sea and we few who remain from the old order must ..." Tracy can't help glancing into the hut and seeing another paunchy man, in the usual grass skirt and a heritage designer T-shirt, dictating to a girl about her own age.

At a pause in her next dictation Tracy, after a nervous giggle, dares to confront Mr. Gray with what she has seen.

"Mr. Gray, you are so good to me and the food and everything here is marvellous, it's all so luxurious – I mean in its basic way, but – I am kind of like lonely. I saw – I couldn't help seeing, I do have to get out sometimes and stroll around a little, not just to the pool – I mean I'm getting overweight even for me – and I couldn't help looking through a door – and I saw –"

"Yes," says Mr. Gray flatly. "I know what you saw. You saw Minister Groggstart dictating to his p.a., Threnody Smythe. She is the only other young woman here." He sighs. "I was hoping this would not happen. It would be very unfortunate if the two of you were to exchange information on the very confidential material you have been asked to transcribe."

"Confidential? I thought it was for speeches you plan to give."

"Speeches, Miss Troutman, are confidential like anything else until the speech is made."

He must be really pissed off, thinks Tracy, he's used my surname. "I'm sorry, I would never never give out any information. I've signed the confidentiality clause at the company and everything – I just thought – maybe she's lonely too – it would be nice if we could like get together."

Mr. Gray sighs again. "Well, okay. It is a bit dull for you, I realise. I will talk to Minister Groggstart and if he agrees you girls can meet."

The next week goes by only a little faster. Threnody, for all her exotic name, is not very talkative or lively. A stiff, serious girl, she is passionately devoted to her unattractive boss, whose praises she incessantly sings. Other than that she seems mainly interested in food and the heady sweet fruit drinks with which they are provided, and in spending a good part of the day asleep, with one of the thin servants fanning her. "Isn't that wonderful? Minister Groggstart says they used to have that when Britain had an empire. Servants fanning. Can you imagine?"

"I wouldn't like it," Tracy says, "having a stranger stand there while I sleep."

"Oh but it's not like if it was a person," Threnody says. "I mean a person like somebody you might know."

Infected by the somnolent lassitude of the island, Tracy begins to lose track of days and of time; without her phone she can only judge time by the height of the sun and the three very satisfying meals brought to her hut every day. The best hour is cocktail, when the skinny servant appears with another amazing tropical concoction, floating rare bits of lemon, orange or olive which seem absolutely real. Where and how did they get all this? Those wonderful drinks were increasing her lassitude. Sometimes she could barely rouse herself when summoned to Mr. Gray's old-fashioned dictation or to receive the manicurist, hair-dresser or make-up artist, more skinny servants, male, female or androgynous, Mr. Gray sends around to see if she could use them. She would say yes to pass the time – but really why when there was no one to look good for? Of course, she must look well when she came back, so she supposed there was that point to it. Still the almost unvaried routine is becoming boring and she is not sorry when she estimates that it must have been nearly two weeks since their arrival and their stay must be coming to an end.

It is just at this point Mr. Gray stops by with an unusually big smile and announces, "Things may be getting a bit dull for you and Threnody (never Threnody, thinks Tracy, she is so boring herself) so you will be pleased to hear that Lord Reclamation is arriving tomorrow and we are to put on a bit of a festival for him. We will have costumes, music, dancing and a barbecue. You and Threnody as the only young women here will be given special costumes and crowned like queens –"

"How can you have a barbecue," Tracy asks. "The food is good but I haven't seen a single locust or anything to grill."

"Ah," says Mr. Gray, smiling more cheerfully still, "We have our ways and means. What our miraculous chef can do with quorn has to be seen to be believed. But here, I have brought your costume. Try it on." Tracy embarrassedly takes the strange garment handed her, a sort of tunic of what – banana leaves, if one could imagine such a thing, "I'll turn around," says Mr. Gray affably, seeing her hesitation, "while you take off your grass skirt."

Tracy obediently removes her fake grass skirt and puts on the strange green tunic. "You can turn around now," she giggles with a last attempt to be inviting.

Mr. Gray beams. "Very becoming," he says, "Very pretty." But he keeps his distance.

"So when is the music and dancing?" Tracy asks, wondering how all these men and indeterminate gender people were going to dance with only two definite girls.

"Later," says Mr. Gray, patting her bare arm with a kind of fatherly affection. "The drinks waiter will bring a really good cocktail to put you in the mood. Then you must rest, and we'll call you and Threnody later. I'm going now to start the fire." He smiles more broadly still and hurries off.

The thin pallid man called the drinks waiter duly appears with what does turn out to be a particularly delicious cocktail. Just before handing it to her, he hesitates and gives her a curious furtive look, as if he wants to say something; then so quickly he almost spills it, he puts down the tray with its tall glass and flees.

Oh well, thinks Tracy, maybe he at least fancies me. Poor bastard. I'd almost have him I'm so frustrated here. Then the drink, almost at once, goes to her head. She feels exalted but strangely drowsy and soon, hearing the first crackle of the fire, she falls asleep, wondering what might be barbecued by Mr. Gray's miraculous chef.

# The Afterthought

It was a lonely house at the edge of a deep dark forest … and that is how dark stories begin.

This however is not a dark story.

It is the story of the happiest summer of my life.

I was the youngest of three children, an accident or an afterthought, perhaps one of those children conceived in an attempt to revive a failing or tedious marriage. My brother was seven years older than I was, my sister nine. They were lively, clever, handsome children, popular at school, doted on by their proud parents. I, the afterthought – for so I actually thought of myself when I became old and literate enough to use such words – was not. If the youngest and last in a family is often the object of particular attention and devotion, this was not my case. I was a thin, frail, timid little boy, with neither talents nor looks to recommend me.

I cannot say that my parents or siblings were ever conspicuously unkind. My sister for a time enjoyed playing the little mother, but soon grew weary of that when the pale anxious baby that was myself did not develop into something that could ever add to her image of healthy vibrant youth but only detract from it. My brother politely ignored me. My parents made the requisite gestures of affection and certainly I never wanted for anything material within their means. Children, however, can sense whether or not they are truly loved.

I accepted this. I did not find myself loveable.

My education was sketchy. When I did attend school I was terrified by the noise, the obstreperousness, the roughness of my fellow pupils. Most of the time I was simply too ill to go. The bullying I somehow expected and dreaded actually happened seldom; I was small and weak enough that teachers were moved to protect me, perhaps also and not least because my parents were prominent people in our town. If I had academic gifts, my frequent absences left no scope to display them. Like many such lonely children, in those mercifully pre-computer and early television days, I became an ardent reader, and there my family deserves my undying gratitude, for ours, whatever it might have lacked, was never a household lacking in books. I devoured the children's classics of my time and country: Bambi, Heidi, the Swiss Family Robinson, Peter's Trip to the Moon, the fairy tales of Andersen and Grimm, and soon graduated to adult books, the Greek myths, the story of Troy, the plays of Schiller and Goethe. Books supposedly cultured people had even if they never read them. I did. And poetry: Heine, Rilke, Hölderlin. And later the novels of Stefan Zweig.

One especially bad winter, my usual winter cough grew worse and before the spring came I had started coughing a little blood. In those deprived post-war days, tuberculosis was rife and still to be feared, but the doctor told my parents not to be alarmed; x-rays revealed nothing dire, just a small shadow on one lung. He prescribed medicine and recommended that as soon as the weather improved I be sent to the country to recuperate in better air. My parents decided against a mountain clinic. They thought that, shy as I was, I would be miserable among strangers; so they settled for hills and woods, my bachelor uncle's gloomy big house at the edge of the Forest of Sonderbar. They had never realised how much I felt my own family as strangers and that a new group of strangers, with the buffer or bond of a common sickness, might actually have been more congenial to their shy child. But children then were not consulted, and it was thought that Uncle's kindly old housekeeper would be an ideal nurse and substitute Mama, and there would be a tutor to give me lessons at home.

So in April, as soon as it could all be arranged, I left for the country.

My uncle came to collect me. I had only met him twice, and formed no opinion about him; I remembered only that he was big, with bushy grey hair and a bushy moustache and that he very often said "Hmmm"; whether in doubt or assent seemed ambiguous. Our journey together and our limited conversation added no colours to this preliminary impression. I was too nervous to take in much of the countryside on our train journey. Trees, houses, farms, horses, cows, churches, telegraph poles, wooded hills ... all went by in a kind of whirl. I was an urban child; I had never been, since I could remember, in real countryside. We were met at the little station by a pony and trap – a pony and trap, very antiquated even for then. Perhaps an eccentricity of my uncle's; at all events, an eccentricity that thrilled me to the bone. My uncle in turn seemed thrilled to forsake forlorn attempts at conversation with me for a hearty chat with the coachman, groom, general factotum as I was to find later, a hearty chat in local dialect about local events. Now, at the pace of the cart, the urban child began to take in his surroundings. Trees, so many trees, not pollarded as in our streets, tall magnificent trees spreading their branches, pines, sycamores, ash trees, flowering chestnuts with white candles of bloom. Little fields, long low farmhouses with smoke curling lazily from their chimneys above roofs of red tiles, with red geraniums in their windows and green benches by their front doors. Then it was all woods, a lane through woods, woods closing around us. We mounted an incline where at last we reached another clearing, and there was the house.

It was not really a very big house but it was imposing because it was so grim. It was a house from what later I was to call the neo-age; neo-Classical, neo-Renaissance, neo-Gothic. The house my uncle had inherited was neo-Gothic; dark stone and half-timbered, arched mullioned windows, a couple of senseless turrets and a strip of duck-pond without ducks that might once have been meant to extend into a moat. My heart sank. Sunshine and much fresh air, the doctor had said. Was this really the place for my cure? Did my parents know – had they ever seen it? But the smell of the wooded air was sweet and sharp and invigorating, and the 'motherly' housekeeper, smelling equally good of apples, starched laundry, and fresh bread, who embraced me as I alighted from the cart, made me feel immediately safe and at home.

My room in the house was cheerful enough. It faced south, had one of the larger windows, and Emma the kind welcoming housekeeper, I was pleased to find, occupied a room immediately next door. If there was anything in the house to match its Gothic exterior the presence of Emma I was sure would banish it. I soon made friends with the rest of the staff, Hans the gruff coachman and gardener, Lise the kitchenmaid, Lotte the cleaner and laundress. The women seemed delighted to have a child in their midst in this lonely house. I was petted as never at home. A wicker chaise-longue was placed on the terrace for me to while away sunny hours, I was asked to name my favourite foods and given them. When any of the staff had a free half hour they sometimes offered to engage me in a game of lotto or checkers.

"You must always be happy here," said Emma, "it will

make you better quickly not ever to sit and brood."

My uncle I saw only at lunchtime. My breakfast was later than his, my supper earlier. He spent his lunch with a newspaper which he read with a lorgnette and frequent hmmm hmmms. He did always ask how I was feeling and if I needed anything and I gave always the same responses; I was feeling well, I lacked for nothing. What my uncle did, where he went, the rest of his days I never learned. Sometimes he disappeared with the pony and trap; sometimes he disappeared on foot, swinging a walking stick or a furled umbrella, depending on the look of the sky. I would have loved to go out in the pony and trap myself with the coachman and maybe be allowed to hold the reins a little but I was too shy to ask.

In the first month of summer I put on weight and colour, as the housekeeper reported to my mother on my mother's weekly phone calls. The local doctor who came every week, a cheerful young man quite different from our doctor at home, was also satisfied with my progress. As for me, my little world was complete, except for two things. I had read and re-read the few favourite books I had brought with me, and my uncle's library, which I had assumed would be something like my parents', seemed to consist of a few gold-tooled leather-bound volumes dealing with philosophy and biblical commentary. Except for newspapers, my uncle was not a reader; the gold-tooled volumes, which I never saw him take off their shelves, were probably part of his inheritance. I did find one fat set of encyclopaedias dealing with the natural world; insects, mammals, sea creatures, but after I took one down, with great difficulty, and struggled with it to a table, I found I did not have the strength to put it back on the shelf and dropped it on my foot when I tried. Emma rushed in, hearing the crash, put the book back for me and said I must not try to lift those books again. Kind as she was, I was too diffident to ask her or the maid to take them down and put them back for me.

The other thing I wished was to walk in the woods. Not just around the manicured garden with its sedate beds of pansies, montbretia, daisies and chrysanthemums, paths of white gravel and little apple trees; but among the great dark trees beyond, where everything whispered and rustled and chirped and called, where the smell of pine needles and bark and leaf mold and moss and rich earth was more vivid and intoxicating than the scent of any garden flower. The scent of adventure, of mystery and the unknown, of something outside my firmly regulated life. And there was a way; beyond the garden gate, was a little faint path that led right into the first grove of trees. It was such a longing that I overcame my shyness and did once ask Emma, "Could we not have a walk in the woods?" "Why ever would we do that, child?" she said. "It is dark in the woods. You need clear air and sunshine." So I gave that up, with the lack of determination with which I usually gave up things, but the longing was so great that I also asked Hans the coachman. With another approach. Did he ever go to cut wood for the stoves, and would he take me? "The woodcutter does all that," said Hans, "why would you want to go into the woods? Children can get lost in the woods and it's all darkness and shade. A boy with your sickness needs warmth and sunshine." Lastly, I tried Lise the maid. "Oh no," she exclaimed, quite startled, "I never go into the woods. My father goes for mushrooms but I never go. You can get lost in the woods and never come out."

Then all at once everything changed.

My uncle was expecting an important visitor, whose titled name was mentioned in hushed voices by the staff. The peaceful somnolence of the house was broken. There was a frenzy of silver-polishing, furniture polishing, pony-grooming, hedge-trimming ... no one had time to play lotto or cards with me. I realised that, as long as I went to bed and appeared at meals at the appointed times, no one now bothered much about what I did or where I was. And I thought, if I open the garden gate and shut it very quietly and go just a little little way to look into the forest ... I could even scatter crumbs like Hansel and Gretel or tie a string to the gate to be sure of my way back – I need not even go out of sight of the gate ... if only I were not so timid ... if only ...

For no one had actually forbidden me to go out of the gate and into the forest. So it would not really be disobedient. Would it? But they *had* said '*You could get lost in the forest and never come out.*'

Obsessive, nervous, scrupulous little boy that I was, I tormented myself with these absurd ditherings. And then, one late afternoon, when all the staff were busy and my uncle in town, as if the forest called me and I had to answer, I did – it sounds ridiculous but it was – the boldest, most independent thing I had ever done in my life.

My trembling fingers, as if of themselves, opened the garden gate and without a glance behind me I walked down the path.

What I saw of the forest from my window was only a fringe. I had barely inhaled the forest, heard its myriad bird calls and little scurrying animal sounds, looked up at the sun-dappled leaves and needles, when the path took me to a clearing, and I was once again in the afternoon light.

I did not see where the path went on, and I knew I must take careful note of where it had entered so I could find it back. As unskilled in orientation as I was in everything else, I was concentrating on this and debating whether I should take off my cap and put it down on the path, when another child came out of the opposite trees.

The child, a thin child like myself, with a shock of pale hair and very blue eyes, dressed as the village people were then, regarded me with wary but friendly curiosity, and then said, "What is your name, little boy?"

"Albert," I stammered.

"Albertli," he said, using at once the diminutive common among friends, which my siblings and parents never used. "Albertli, are you from the big house?"

"Yes," I said faintly.

"Albertli, I'm Simon. Would you like to play with us?"

Us, I wondered. My shyness made me stammer, "I – I – d-don't know many games –"

"We always play just one game. We will teach you. " He turned to the forest behind him and called "Come out, everyone. I have found Albertli, a new little boy, and he will play with us. Come out, come out!"

One by one, other boys and girls emerged from the trees, all dressed in the same simple clothes, all of different ages, the youngest perhaps four, the oldest perhaps eleven, two years older than myself. They were smiling but silent, compared to the noisy pupils at school. Two of them took my hands, all the other hands were joined, and we began to dance in a ring, first left, then right, and the children began singing, over and over, the same little rhyme. "Man of Black, don't touch my back. Man of Black, don't touch my back." That was easy enough; I sang too. The dance became faster and faster, everyone was laughing – then suddenly the dance stopped, the hands dropped, and Simon turned to me and said, "Now we all line up. The littlest one first, then the next littlest, on up to the tallest. And then we count.

And so we find the number nine and number nine is the Man of Black."

We were lined up, and with more laughing and jostling number nine was pulled out of the row and the others dispersed. Then two of the older ones, quite serious now, marked off a territory in the clearing, a kind of triangle. A stick with my cap perched on it was one apex. The others were trees, designated by little heaps of stones placed at their feet. Another stick with another cap on it, inside the triangle was the goal.

"That is *his* ground," Simon explained. "Now we go into the trees and we tiptoe out. We try to reach the goal before the Man of Black can catch us. Whoever he catches has to help him catch the rest until all are caught."

"Are they always all caught?" my meticulous anxious self wanted to know.

"Oh yes of course. Always. Once he has caught two or three it is easy for them to catch the rest."

The children vanished into the trees, as silently and swiftly as they had come. I followed them. Number Nine stood proudly in the centre of his triangle. "Are you afraid of the Black Man?" he called loudly, taunting the players.

"No," shouted four children from the woods, and crept forward into the dangerous triangle. Number Nine moved back a little to draw them in further.

"What do you do when the Black Man comes?" he called again. "What do you do when the Black Man comes?"

The children ventured more into the triangle, and while the Man of Black's attention was on them three others tiptoed into the triangle from another grove of trees. "We take to our legs," shouted the first lot, laughing, and ran out of the triangle; but meanwhile the Man of Black had seen the others who hoped to escape his attention, and with a rapid graceful turn swooped down on them and touched one shoulder before the little girl could escape.

The game went on until every child was caught. I was one of the last, not due to my skill at escaping but my timidity. Next time, I told myself, I will be bolder. Next time? Would there be a next time?

"We must all go back now," Simon said. "But we will play again tomorrow. Will you come, Albertli?"

"Yes, oh yes. Albertli must come. Come tomorrow, Albertli," the children chorused.

"Of course I will come. I have been so happy –" then blushing and feeling I was saying too much, I added shakily. "I want very much to come. If I can get away."

"You must come," said Simon. "We will wait for you. But do not tell them in the big house that you play with us."

"Of course not," I said without thinking, feeling intuitively that these children and this game, maybe because from their very old-fashioned clothes and a thinness surprising with their amazing energy, were village children who would not have met with the approval of my uncle and his staff.

Before the children disappeared into the woods from which they had come, one of them gave me back my cap which had been used for marking the Man of Black's territory, and led me to the path.

The next day I managed to sneak off into the woods again. And the next, and any day without rain, any time after my obligatory post-lunch nap, that I could manage it. Sometimes I pretended to still be asleep when Emma came in with a cup of tea; sometimes I left an open book on the chaise-longue on the terrace so it would appear I had just gone to the old-fashioned chain-pull 'water closet' as Emma still called it, or back upstairs to fetch something from my bedroom. I became cunning, fleet-footed, evasive, hypocritical. As children can, to get what they want most in the world. The game was like an addiction – you might even say the game was an addiction. The game and the strange children were the centre of my life.

One day, reading on my chaise-longue, I found myself humming and then singing "Man of Black, don't touch my back. Man of Black, don't touch my back" just as Emma the housekeeper came to bring me a cup of tea. "What is it you are singing?" asked Emma, her face without its usual greeting smile.

"It's a song from a game," I said, and quickly added. "A game some of the children played at school."

"How strange," said Emma musingly. "I didn't think children in the towns played that game any more. It used to be played in the village; but I haven't seen it since I myself was a child."

I thought it better to say no more. I buried myself in my oft-read book, and bit my tongue to remind myself not to sing the song again.

The game was hectic and fast and wildly exciting. But the children who played it were totally unlike the rough children in my school playground. No one pushed or hit, cheated or hurled abuse or swore. The Man of Black's tap on the back was merely that, never anything that might knock you off your feet, and although their thin fingers would curl around mine when we held hands for the round dance that began the game, those fingers were gentle and soft as leaves.

It was not always the same children who came to play. There were some who came nearly every time, others who came less often; had it not been like that, it would always have been the same child who was number nine and the Man of Black until the children grew bigger. I thought about this, and wondered if by next summer I might be bigger and the row changing a little so I could be – for I longed to be – myself the Man of Black.

I did not know there was to be no next summer, and the present summer was coming to an end.

It was soon time for school again, and the tutor engaged to give me lessons appeared at the door, a charmless, obsequious young man, armed with schoolbooks, rulers, pencils, maps and not with any love for his profession or real interest in the hapless pupil on whom it was to be exercised.

He had been told I was fragile and not to overtax me, but he set me so much preparation for lessons, and he spent so much time in the house, that my sacred hours in the woods became impossible without open defiance and discovery, which I knew I could not risk.

Once or twice I thought, in those miserable afternoons, I heard little voices calling me from the forest. "Albertli, Albertli, come! We miss you." And once I thought, or imagined, Simon saying, "Come Albertli; come and even if you are not number nine we will let you be the Man of Black."

This was the point in my life where a kind, intelligent and inspiring teacher could have saved me. The teacher I had was devoid of those qualities. He was deferent to my uncle or the mention of my uncle, he was polite to the staff, but I felt a strong undercurrent of resentment whenever he was alone with me, irritation with my slowness and absent-mindedness, resentment that this weakly ungifted child was what he needed to earn his living. I think if I had not been ill and my uncle and parents had countenanced it, he would have been happy to beat me, as was still the custom in my childhood. Bereft of my companions, the dear children of the woods, and delivered to his boring routines, I rapidly got worse again. After much medical consultation, I was sent away from my uncle's house, to go briefly home and then after all to a sanatorium. The servants kissed me and wept; I wept too, and as the pony and trap pulled away on the drive past the forest, I listened in vain for those beloved voices I was never to hear again.

I spent three years in the sanatorium, years actually happier than my previous years at home. I did have some company, I did make a few friends. But never was anyone as dear to me as the children in that enchanted wood; and not a day went by that I did not think of them, although some instinctive caution kept me from telling anyone ever about those children and the game we had played in the hidden clearing at the end of the path. I longed, I hoped, to go back again to my uncle's house and find them. It was not to be. While I was in the sanatorium, my uncle died, and the house was sold to pay unsuspected substantial debts – to the bitterness of my mother, his nearest relation, who had hoped that she or her children might after all come into something when her much older brother died.

So I never went back to the dear old house with the ludicrous turrets and mullioned panes, I never saw Emma, Lotte, Hans or the strange village children again. The memory of the game in the forest remained for a while vivid and fresh, and I developed an odd little habit of reciting the verse from the round dance whenever I felt anxious or lonely or thwarted. *"Man of Black don't touch my back! Man of Black don't touch my back!"* I would say to myself and somehow it seemed to help. Then there were new challenges, new pursuits, the sickly child did recover and become an adult, and that summer became distant and unreal, like a happy dream.

When I was well enough to live in the world again things did not go too badly. My avid reading, my thirst for knowledge, were rewarded; I did get through university and was able to work, as a librarian among the books I loved and, I hope, I encouraged some of that love in others. I never married nor, to my knowledge, fathered a child; I had a few friends, a few favourite haunts, a ground floor apartment with a bit of garden, a cat, a book collection of my own ... I was content. The cat, the latest cat, grew old and died. I too was growing old so she was not replaced. My two closest friends soon died too, and my own health deteriorated. The early tuberculosis had left me vulnerable; weak lungs, failing heart. Once more I was timid, frail and lonely; I had not anticipated that when you are old you can become not only childish again but become the child you outgrew – the child you thought in adulthood you had overcome. It was then I suddenly longed to see, before it was too late, the place where I had spent those extraordinary dreamlike weeks. I took a train to the little station at Semmelringen and a taxi with an old taxi driver who fortunately knew from my description what once had been my uncle's estate and was now a development of commuters' three-story apartment houses, with its own little supermarket, allotments, kindergarten, restaurant and café.

Those as old as I am and with any memory left do not need the statistics and computer models of science to know that the earth we depend on is near collapse. All the evidence we need is before our eyes. We have seen the peaceful streams of our childhood metamorphose into torrential floods after exceptional – then no longer exceptional – rains, we have seen once pristine sands covered in plastic and oil, we have seen little farms fertilized by cow-dung and compost turned into vast fields of monocrops that exhaust and never replenish their once healthy soil. So the disappearance of my uncle's house and the spreading suburbia that covered what had been his land and the woods beyond was no surprise. The surprise was that a clearing remained; a clearing the size of the ancient one that had been in the forest not far from the garden gate; a clearing with gravel paths, tidy flower beds, clipped hedges just like my uncle's formal garden except that in its centre was a memorial stone with a plaque. This little park was a memorial garden, the plaque explained, dedicated to the dead of the two great world wars and also to the victims of the last cholera epidemic in 1872.

So, I thought, they have left something; surely this was the clearing I knew – but why a little memorial garden in the middle of the houses rather than more allotments or a playing field? And the children I had played with, were any of them still living in the area, and could I find out? I had never known their surnames, and there must have been dozens of Lottes and Lisas and Rudis and Simons … still, there would be a local parish record of births and deaths, and I was suddenly in a fever to find out.

The clerk at the city hall listened to my story and told me to come back the next day after he had had time to consult the records. When I returned, he greeted me with a puzzled air. "When you were a child here, there were almost no other children in the village. Only the old people. And you say that in the woods you were sometimes a dozen or even more? Children in those days when they were not in school had to help their parents on the farms. And as I remember it, they were warned off the woods, because it was so easy to get lost." He hesitated. "Sometimes it is hard to remember correctly things in our childhood –"

"No," I said indignantly. "I do not have a failing memory, at least not yet. Day after day I played with those children. We always played the same game. I know it was an old game. It was called, Who's Afraid of the Man of Black –"

The clerk said abruptly, "No, whatever you saw, I can do no more to help you. But I think you should talk to Father Florian, the old priest."

Father Florian looked so old and so much more frail than myself that I wondered if his memory would be up to dealing with my question, but I told my story again, and asked why there was a memorial garden among all those new apartment houses. Father Florian listened as attentively as he could; his head wobbled, his shaking hands frequently pulled out a handkerchief to wipe his dripping nose. When I finished, the shaking right hand made a cross on his chest; but when he spoke his voice was firmer than his hands, and what he said was simply, "The children you played with were all dead."

For a few moments I was dizzy and a wave of darkness washed over my eyes. Could I have heard right? I gripped the arms of my chair to steady myself, and the old priest stretched out his shaking hand to steady me also. Then seeing I was recovering, he used the hand to make another sign of the cross. I stammered – "What did you say?"

He repeated it in the same flat, steady, matter-of-fact voice.

"You – you mean they were ghosts – but that is not possible – I don't even believe in ghosts – and they were real – they were physical – they touched me – they took my hands –"

"There are more things in heaven and earth…" said the old priest.

"Then – real or ghosts – who were they?"

The old priest sighed. "They were children who died in the last great epidemic. The game you played was invented after an earlier plague. The Man of Black is Death. The clearing in the woods where you played was a plague graveyard; there were too many for the cemetery and people feared infection, so victims were sometimes buried in a mass grave and with flimsy markings. Later, no one remembered or perhaps chose to say where exactly this graveyard was. When the new houses were built, after your uncle's land was sold, the bones were discovered and reburied. The last cholera killed many children in the village, so those would be the children who played with you. No one wanted to live in a house built on that ground, so it was turned into a memorial park. The woods where you played were feared by the villagers, and children were warned never to go into them alone. No living child would have gone there to play with you. Two children who did go alone to the woods never came back and were never found."

"That – that – cannot have been due to those children – the children I knew – they were so gentle and kind and – no, no they must have been real – and whoever – or whatever they were I cannot believe they ever meant me ill –"

The old priest shook his doddering head. "Perhaps not. But playing games with the dead," he smiled, he was not without humour, the shaky old priest, "is never a safe activity. And some of the old villagers would have said that there are ghosts sent by the devil, ghosts who want your soul ... of course no one now believes in the devil. Still, I think it is fortunate that you went away from your uncle's house when you did."

I left the old priest's house stunned and shaken, and took the train back that very night. There was no point in revisiting what once had been a clearing in a dense forest. Whatever magic it had held was dead and buried as surely as victims of the vanished plagues.

When I was calmer at last, I tried to absorb what the

priest had told me. It was not possible. It could not be true. But the records confirmed what he said. And if there were such – ghosts, such things as that – a lonely sensitive sickly child would have been their likely companion – or prey – No. Living or spirits, I could never believe those children meant me harm.

And after all my tormented musings, I know one thing for certain. I was never again as happy as I was that summer with them.

I am very old now, very alone. The Man of Black who comes to us all is waiting for me. I think very often about that idyllic summer, and sometimes I find myself saying, as other people near the end of life might say their prayers, I find myself saying some of the children's names –

Simi, Rudi, Steffi, Conrad, Anni, Lotti, Robi, Resi, Marilli

Whoever, whatever, wherever you are –

*I am not afraid of the Man of Black*

Whenever I hear you call me again, I will come.

## I Say Goodnight But Not Goodbye

This story is written, with thanks and fond memories, for my dear friend the late W. Pendleton Campbell, who pointed out to me in a country churchyard the tombstone bearing that strange legend, a stone that was just slightly raised at one end.

Like the name 'Lycanthrope House' which inspired another story, I was never able, on repeated visits, to find the tomb again.

"So why are we stopping here?"

Jeremy, the fastest of the four walkers, dropped his rucksack impatiently down on a tomb. "Why are we stopping," he called back to the others. "There was nothing in the village, no pub, no café, nowhere even to fill a water bottle – "

The path had led them through a picturesque but neglected and totally quiet village to a small church, almost invisible in a huddled grove of trees, its stubby tower and dark roof barely rising above the conifers that lined the crumbling churchyard wall. Like a whale-back rising out of a sinister restless sea, thought Penelope, the last walker, who was fond of similies.

Jeremy, awaiting an answer and seeing the tomb under his sack had one end just slightly raised and an inscription, a single very clear line, read the inscription out loud. *"I say goodnight but not goodbye."* "Hey," said Jeremy, amused, "Here's a joker trying to get out." But no one was listening; Jeremy's sister Jess, organiser and leader of this rambling quartet, was consulting her *Guide to St Ursula's Way.* Jeremy repeated his question, "So why do we want to stop here?"

"It says we shouldn't miss the silkie sculptures in the church."

"God, you and your St Ursula book. So what's a silky when it's at home?"

"It's a human that can become a seal. Or a seal that can become human. It's an old legend. Anyway, it's not just sculpture, it's a whole – like a collage – or installation – or so Google says." Tony, Jess's boyfriend, always seemed to know more than anyone else about the things they came across.

"How can there be an in-sta-llation," Jeremy drawled the word, "in a church?"

"It's to raise money for church restoration. Come on everybody, it's by somebody famous, we might as well have a look."

Jess went to the old oak door. Above it, a pop-eyed gargoyle stuck out its tongue at her, another gazed down past its elephantine nose, a third, grinning, displayed its long wicked incisors. Jess grasped the green-stained iron ring latch, which refused to turn. "I'll go round the side. There might be another door."

"Little churches don't have two doors," said Penelope in an undertone. She looked up at the gargoyle and shivered, thinking, 'I don't like this place. Why does Jess have to see everything? We're on a long-distance walk, we should be setting a pace –'

Meanwhile, Jeremy pointed out the strange tombstone to Tony, who said, "I bet we can find some more weird ones. Look, right next to it, on this very old tall one, there's this:"

*Let worms, corruption and decay*
*This mortal flesh refine*
*Until on that triumphant day*
*It shall once more be mine*

"After worms, corruptions and decay, I don't think you'd want it back," Jeremy grinned. Penelope chimed in. "It wasn't funny to them. They really believed that, people then. That on Judgement Day they'd get up again and be made whole."

Tony and Jeremy exchanged raised-eyebrow glances. Penelope had been invited by Jess, a friend but not a close one, to make up numbers and as a possible companion for Jeremy who was, for all his boisterousness, recovering with difficulty from a broken relationship. The scheme was not a success; it was soon obvious to the others that Penelope, who frequently winced discreetly when Jeremy spoke, found Jeremy loud, insensitive and vulgar, and that Jeremy found Penelope a pedant and a bore.

Jess was back, shaking her head. "No other way in."

"So much for that," said Jeremy. "Aren't these country churches supposed to welcome the wayfarer – like us? Us pilgrims for St Ursula? Does your precious guide not give opening times? Come on, now that we've stopped, I want to see this damned art work. Can't we rustle up some guardian or something to let us in?"

Just then, as if by magic, one appeared.

He was a plump, balding, very little man, obviously the local vicar – but no, he was dressed not like a vicar but like a priest, in a shabby but flowing cassock of black, and he had a monk's tonsure of sparse remaining hair. He moved with a clanking sound; no doubt, thought the walkers, he carried the keys which would open the thick oak door.

"Good evening, good evening." The little man spoke in a soft husky voice. "Forgive my croaking. Laryngitis, you know. Always happens this time of year. Change of season, you know, and seasons askew, climate askew. Oh yes, oh yes. You are walking young people? Oh yes, many walkers come. St Ursula Major way. The old pilgrims' way. And you would like to see the silkie art? Oh yes, oh yes. I am happy to admit you."

He inserted a key and the door slowly opened, with indignant creaks of its ancient hinges. As he switched on lights, the walkers followed him in.

The church still had its old ebony pews and a granite font whose crudely carved, simple plant motif showed its antiquity. The little vicar, priest, whatever he was, went into his spiel, an automatic spiel the visitors guessed poured forth whether or not required or desired. They should notice, please, the fine barrel vaulting, still original; the church was built in the $12^{th}$ century but much restored, poorly restored, in the $19^{th}$. And also please, some of the carved ends of the ebony pews, crude but also fine, if they would follow him, please, here was a jester, here a fish, symbol of the Christ of course but strangely a fish with two heads facing in opposite directions and here was a very strange carving, a robed figure with a bird-like head, like an Egyptian god, now who would expect that in a small Cornish church?

"But where's the famous silky thing then?" Jeremy was impatient again.

"Ah. The silkie. The silkie is not ancient at all. To raise funds for our much-needed restoration it was decided to allow modern artists to display work in the church, a different one every six months, but this - silkie – (he bit off the word as if to show contempt) has had so much publicity and been nominated for so many prizes that we have now kept her – or him – or it – or alas as modern parlance has it, with no distinction of gender or number, however singular or plural the object, as *they* may be – " He paused briefly but only Penelope caught the pun, and he hurried on. "The silkie is really what they call – an installation. A scattering of pieces and bits. A game of hide and seek. A game of transformations. You must look for the silkie all over the church. Here a flipper, there a hand, a human head, a seal's head. There are seven objects in all and whenever you do find one, we ask you to drop a coin – a coin of your choice, a penny will do – though of course larger coins not to mention bills are very welcome indeed –" He paused to draw breath. "The objects are of course removable and will go back to the artist when the exhibit is over. I understand there is already a prestigious collector interested in this installation, oh yes, which is why sadly it is important to keep the church locked as the objects are – objects of value. Whatever we may think. Value. Oh yes."

"I've found one," cried Jeremy. "There's a flipper behind the altar. No – I mean it looks like a flipper. I guess it's really –" he was examining it – "it's just a rubber glove cut and stitched together and stuffed so it looks like – really, is this the great guy's work that somebody's going to pay through the nose – the seal's nose for? It looks pretty amateurish. I mean, a kid could have done this."

"I have one too," called Jess. "It's two praying human hands. Here, behind this pew. Does that really fit – I mean, believing in silkies must be a pagan thing –"

"She, he, it could be praying to be turned back into a seal," said Jeremy, getting into the spirit of the objects.

"But how do they all fit together?" Penelope wondered.

"They don't," said Tony. "The guy told you. It's all bits and pieces. They don't have to make a complete – creature."

Jess was reading a pamphlet she had found. "It's like a collage, really, like those hands are taken from a nineteenth century tomb. The artist didn't make most of the things. He just collected them."

"I have another one," said Jeremy, "and God only knows what this one is. It looks like the arse end of a kid's rubber duck, but it's been painted to look like – I guess like the snout of a seal."

They continued their game of finding the artist's *objets trouvés.* Lying on a pew a sealskin coat, stuffed and shaped and sewn to resemble a seal body. A woman's nude, armless torso – a dressmaker's dummy with a painted navel and nipples, and a painting on the back like a tattoo of a fish. And another pair of hands with the beatifically open extended palms of the welcoming Christ, taken this time from an old wooden carving.

"What do they do with these things," Jess wanted to know, "when there's a service?"

"We put them in the refectory. Yes, the refectory. Then we put them back. And there are not many services here any more."

"We've had a snout, one flipper, two pairs of hands, two bodies. It doesn't make much anatomical sense," said Tony.

"Transformations, you see. Transformation. Do not need even numbers. It all comes mysteriously together in the end. Together in the mind of the beholder. Oh yes, so the artist says. How he explains. There is another leaflet, by the artist, for twenty pee." Jess, who had been scanning the leaflet, put it back.

It was Penelope who found the last object.

Suddenly weary, and tired of what she thought was a silly game and an even sillier and yes, she felt somehow blasphemous, art work and fund-raising scheme, she sat down on a pew and tried in vain to capture some of the antique peace that little country churches like this one should hold inside their walls. Penelope was not religious but her parents were, and she had been brought up with a lingering sense of the sacred and of, simply, the fitness of things; what her grandparents would have called good taste. She fixed her eyes on the kneeling cushion at her feet; such 'kneelers' were usually embroidered by women of the parish, sometimes with a very skilful and pretty petit point. This one was almost as bizarre as the silkie installation; a bleeding heart of Jesus, surrounded by a pattern of red gore in concentric, broken circles, like a maze. She turned to look at the cushion on its left, a Sebastian pierced by arrows. And the one to its right, a spiny circular pattern with red spots, and a brown oval in the centre. With a start, she realised what it was; Christ's head with its crown of thorns, seen from above. Why were – why would – the serene pious old ladies Penelope had always pictured as embroiderers be making cushions like these? Penelope got up, and as she did noticed something else under the pew in front of her, and bent to pick it up. It was a sculpted human head, made from some light material, a girl's head, with wide goggle eyes and fish's mouth, sucked in at the corners, like a mouth gasping for breath.

"I've found a head," she announced, but the others were all laughing about something and no one paid attention except the priest. He moved closer to her and said softly, "Grotesque, is it not? I find the things grotesque. Not proper for a church. Oh no, not proper. But times have changed and the elders – the bishops – say we must have restoration money or our churches will fall apart. Or be deconsecrated and sold. To retired bankers perhaps who will make them into holiday homes. Oh yes, oh yes, that is how they go. What will happen to these beautiful pews, the beautiful vaulting, the old tombs? God knows. God alone knows. The altar will be a cocktail bar –"

"Surely they would take out the altar," interrupted Penelope.

"Not if the new owner pays enough. Money is everything now. Everything," the little man exclaimed bitterly, fluttering his black sleeves.

"Hey," said Jeremy, "What's that deep conversation

over there? Penny, have you found something?"

"I've found a head. I already said so but no one heard me."

"A head? Oh good on you, Penny, that's number seven. Move over, let us see. Gosh, that's weird. I guess she's about to turn into a seal? Or trying not to?"

Penelope and the priest exchanged smiles. Penelope thought again of the cushions. They too were not normal. There's something wrong here and he, the little priest, vicar, whatever he is, understands. I wish I could talk more to him, alone.

As if reading her mind, the little man suddenly burst into speech, but it was a speech addressed to them all, in a still husky but louder voice than he had used before. "I am condemned. Oh yes, condemned to show you these new things, these ugly things devoid of faith. Oh yes. I am condemned for my sins. We need the donations. We need the money. Without the donations of travellers such as you this beloved little church is also condemned. I would like to dwell on the beauty of the old carvings. The carvers were nameless. They worked not for the crowd's adulation, not for prizes, not only for money. They worked for the glory of God. But I am condemned to show you – these." His black sleeves swept back in a gesture of contempt. "And," he added more softly, "to ask you for your donations."

The impassioned speech left him breathless and the young people embarrassed, except for Penelope. "I'm sure we understand," she said and moved quickly to search for her wallet in the rucksack she had left on a pew.

Somewhat reluctantly, the others followed suit.

Once outside again, with the heavy oak door shut behind them, they all felt relief to be back in the gentle air of the country afternoon, even though the sun was much lower – could they have been that long in the church? Consulting watches or smartphones, they realised more than an hour of daylight had been lost. "Shit," said Jeremy, "Now we've got to hurry to make that hostel at St Ursula Major in time to get supper and decent beds."

The old man in black hovered nearby, listening, and at once put in, "The path is changed ahead. It will not show in your book or your map. It happened only last month. Oh yes, a great piece of cliff has fallen into the sea. Climate change. Oh yes, so many great storms, the cliffs are crumbling. There was such a crash we heard it here. Here in the village. The path now goes over the moor. It is a bad path and there is bog. It is dangerous if the mist draws in. I can take you through the bog; but it would be better to go in the morning when you will be safe alone."

"Of course – the storms. I should have thought. I should have checked," Jess consulted the map. Jeremy, impatient again, said, "Are we going to get your lecture on climate change – just twelve years to save the planet and all that? Twelve years before we die?"

"It's less now," said Jess, and "and it's not a joke. So just shut up, Jeremy." She turned back to the map. "St Ursula Major is only three miles from here. It won't be even near dark yet."

"The mist will come," the old man said. "Oh yes, the mist from the bog. Always the mist. But I can go with you. Only until you have passed the bog."

"Don't you have to stay here," asked Jeremy, "in case anyone else turns up to see the very famous installation? And to guard the church?"

As if reminded, the priest turned back and appeared to lock the door – which was strange, thought Jess, because one didn't hear the key turn. But weren't things strange here altogether?

"No one will come now." the priest answered. "Not

now. Not this evening. No one will come. It is already too late." Then he repeated, "I can take you through the bog. I know the ways through the bog. For many years I have known those ways. Or you can stay here. There is a guest house not far – oh yes, Mrs Termagenton – oh yes, I believe that is her name. Mrs Termagenton. She has two rooms. It is simple but clean. And not dear. Not dear at all."

Aware that Penelope, who after all she had invited, was being given scant attention, Jess went to consult her. But it's her fault too, thought Jess. She's not very forthcoming and Jeremy always seems to annoy her. "Penny, what do you think?"

Before Penelope could answer, Tony chimed in. "I bet as usual there are just double beds. And I'm not spending another night with Jeremy. He not only snores, he kicks and turns all night."

"Hang on," said Jess. "You can hardly expect Penelope..."

"Why not?" Jeremy interrupted. "Hey Penny, how about it? Boy, she looks horrified at the prospect of a night with me. Listen, don't worry, I'll let you have the bed and I'll put my sleeping bag on the floor. Unless we do find a pub and get very merry and we both change our minds." He gave Penelope a mocking leer and added, sotto voce, "You know, Penny, you're not half bad. You're just not very friendly."

"Jeremy, stuff it," Jess said sharply. Then, to Penelope, "Just ignore him. So what do you think?"

"I think we should go. It's light for a couple more hours, I guess, and if the priest – the vicar – goes with us till we're past the bog –"

"Okay then," said Tony, "Go with our little guide here, or stay? Shall we take a vote? All in favour of staying say aye."

The two men said instant ayes. Jess hesitated, then

turned again to Penelope. "I'm sorry Jeremy's being such a prat. Don't worry, he's harmless, even more harmless than he'd like to think. Anyway, you and I will share a room."

"No." Penelope's voice was small and tight. "It's not Jeremy. I don't like this place. I don't like the church, I don't even like these trees, and it isn't just those ghastly – what are they – art objects – and did you see the cushions – the cushions to kneel on – all martyrs and blood – why would old ladies embroidering cushions for church do pictures full of gore? There's something wrong here. Something weird going on. I think we should leave."

Jess sighed and turned to the men. "I'm not leaving," Jeremy said. "It's silly to leave tonight. We should at least check out this place in the village, and then decide."

"By then it'll be too late to go," said Jess.

"No, no." The priest was listening intently to their conversation. "You need only go back to the road and turn left up the next lane. It's five minutes from here."

Tony and Jeremy went and were actually back in less than ten minutes. "It's fine." Jeremy was triumphant. "The old bird's a bit doddery but the rooms look okay, though judging by her surprise at seeing us she hasn't had a guest in years. She even has a girl coming in the morning who can get us breakfast, and there *is* a pub about a mile away. So Bates Motel it's not. How about it? Penelope? Jess?"

"It sounds okay," said Jess.

"I still think we should go," said Penelope.

"*I* think you're outvoted," said Jeremy.

"Oh, I don't care about the votes. You didn't look at the cushions, you didn't pick up that awful – that awful human fish-head – there's something wrong here – and you say the old woman probably hasn't had a guest in years – and if this – this awful installation is famous – why do you think that is?" Penelope was almost tearful.

"Oh God," said Tony. "She's getting one of those bad vibrations."

Penelope's vibrations were well known to Jess and Tony, as was her stubbornness; meek and shy though she is, thought Tony, once she's got an idea into her head there is no getting it out. She's still scared of Jeremy, stupid girl, thought Jess, scared and embarrassed about being scared, this was a lousy idea, I should never have asked her to come.

As for Penelope, she did not at that point know exactly what she thought, only that she wanted to get away from the place and away from the group and, like Jess, that she should never have come.

The little priest, who was still listening intently, cleared his throat, and then said abruptly, "If the young lady wishes to go on and the rest of you wish to stay – I can escort her to St Ursula Major. If she wishes. Once she is past the bog she will be quite safe if she continues alone. Oh yes. Quite safe."

"I don't know," said Jess. "Is that – is that really – do you want to do that, Penny?"

"Oh yes. If the priest – if this gentleman would be so kind – yes."

Jess sighed. "Okay. I'll phone the hostel and tell them to expect you but the rest of us not till tomorrow. But Penny – are you sure?"

"Yes." Penelope's voice was now firm.

"Since the landslide I often guide walkers," the priest said. "I have had kind letters, kind thanks. And many donations for our fund. But we should leave now. I must not be away too long."

When they were gone, it was strangely and suddenly Jeremy who had qualms.

"Maybe we shouldn't have let Penny take off with that creepy little guy. Suppose he's a nutcase? Suppose he attacks her?"

"He's a priest," said Tony. "Priests go after little boys, not women in their twenties nearly two feet taller. Anyway he's not a priest, he's a clergyman. He probably has a wife and ten kids."

"That never stops rapists," said Jeremy.

"Oh for fuck's sake." This from Tony, always the sensible one. "We've all seen them leave together. How could he do anything? She insisted on going, didn't she? And she's an adult, isn't she? So we let her go. So let's not worry about it. And now I think we should find that pub."

Penny, feeling wonderfully released as soon as they were over a hill and out of sight of the church and its crowding, whispering trees, was chatting with her companion.

"I see you agree that this so-called art work does nothing for the atmosphere of the church."

"Oh yes, oh yes. Blasphemy. I call it blasphemy. But we need money, everyone needs money, everything is money. In my day it was not so. The Almighty was the Almighty and a church was a church and art was art."

"When was your day? Have you always been in this parish?"

"Oh yes, oh yes. From birth to death. Two hundred years."

"You mean, your family."

"Oh yes, my family. Yes, we were always in this parish. After we came long long ago, from the far north, across the water. Always here. We knew nothing else. And the youngest son – because we were many – always for the church."

"Did you then perhaps – not wish for the priesthood?"

Penelope was finding herself speaking in the old-fashioned, stilted manner of the old man himself.

"Oh yes. Oh yes. It was as well as anything. But we were not consulted. We followed our elders. Theirs was the final word. Always the final word."

The little priest was walking very fast now, amazingly fast, thought Penelope, for someone so small and so much older – or was he really so old, with his very rotund face it was difficult to tell his age – and he seemed to disregard the flapping cassock which brushed against branches and brambles on the narrow path but never seemed to snag.

The path became steeper and rockier, requiring real concentration; and Penelope longed for some respite to take in this landscape, but felt she could not delay the priest's return. Soon breathless, she no longer spoke, but the little priest continued to mutter to himself – "Soon back – soon – must hurry – not much time."

"Why are we in such a hurry?" Penelope asked at last.

"Must pass the bog before the mist comes down."

"I thought you knew the way, even in the mist."

"Yes. But I must hurry on my return. Only allotted time. Only leave when called."

"But – what do you mean? Who called you?"

"You," said the priest. "You called me. You were not like the others. You were ready to go alone. And you were the one who saw – who saw the blasphemy. Oh yes, the blasphemy."

"You mean – that awful so-called art work? And the – gory cushions?"

"Yes, oh yes. But not the cushions. In the times of the Saviour there was much blood. Much sacrifice. But not all victims – not all sacrifice – is made with blood. But the ladies – the church ladies – are simple ladies, they know only blood. That is why – they stitch – the tapestries."

The path levelled out and seemed to have brought them, without transition, into a different countryside. Penelope had expected the bog would be in a place of pools and reeds and long grasses, but where they reached stepping stones, and then a boardwalk, they were among shrubs and stunted, twisted willows, and the ground looked quite normal, as if one could easily step off the stones and wander among the widely spaced trees.

"We are coming to the boardwalk now. Oh yes, oh yes," said the priest, "and as I foretold the mist is beginning."

"I'm confused," gasped Penelope, still struggling to keep up with him and to keep her balance on the stones and then on the narrow boardwalk, which looked quite old and worn, as far as she could see in the gathering mist, not like something put up recently because of a path diversion. "Which direction is the sea?"

The priest flapped his sleeve vaguely to the left, and then began muttering again. "We must take care here. Oh yes. Great care. The bog here looks harmless but it is not. In minutes it will be over your head. Very deep, the bog. Very deep. In such bogs in the north they found the bog people. Maidens. In the bog. Some are careless, some fall. But some think these were not fallen but – they were victims of a pagan religion. Sacrifice. Not all sacrifice is made with blood."

Penelope was nervous now. "Please," she called, the wavering, mist-shrouded figure ahead, "Please, don't go so fast. I can't keep up. Please wait. I can hardly see my way."

"Dreadful, this paganism, this blasphemy," muttered the priest. Then, louder, "Keep walking, hurry, the mist is coming. The planks are narrow here. Step carefully. The mist comes thicker now. Oh yes, oh yes."

"Please. Wait! I can't go so fast. I can't see." But the

flapping black cassock, more and more shrouded in mist, moved even faster, was soon almost lost to sight. Penelope, terrified now, uncertain whether to still follow or go back, and as she half-turned a plank tipped beneath her and she landed in the bog, and the bog, the innocent looking bog, was at once nearly up to her thighs. She reached desperately for the nearest twigs; they were weak and tore in her clenching fingers, weak, far too weak to hold against the bog. "Come back," she screamed, "come back. Please, please help me."

There was now no one to help. The black figure was now too far ahead or dissolved in the thickening mist, and indeed it was dissolved, its allotted time was up. Before it vanished altogether its voice remained, quite close to Penelope's poor struggling form. "I said good-night but not good-bye" the voice said softly and those were the last words Penelope heard before the bog closed her gasping mouth and flowed into her ears.

## From reviews of other Oliver Books

**The Tourist Season:**
'...a book that demands to be read and savoured carefully, and ... lingers in the mind. This, it seems to me, is simply because Frances Oliver does it all so well ... A perceptive and skilful novel.

The Financial Times

**Xargos:**
'... if a book lives up to the pleasure of the blurb writer's promise that's a real bonus ... the heroine of Frances Oliver's XARGOS turns out to be not only 'beautiful, sexy and inept' but also, in her radiantly self-absorbed way, entirely credible. I greatly enjoyed this intelligent, skilfully organised novel.

Norman Shrapnel, The Guardian

'This is a splendid short novel about the perils of igno-rance (or innocence if one wants to be kinder) written with a nice wit, sharp ear for good dialogue, and some fine, evocative descriptions of Turkey.

Nina Bawden, Daily Telegraph

**The Peacock's Eye:**
'The quality of Frances Oliver's cosmopolitan novels has been insufficiently celebrated. Her writing is both interest-ing - one actually finds things out from it - and intelligent. Her characters speak and think their way through complex moral, emotional and political problems ...
Nabokov said of his invented creature Shade, the author of the poem of Pale Fire, "He is the best of invented poets." - This is still true, but Frances Oliver's translations of Hans Handelbein's poetry are quite impressive. It takes guts for a novelist to invent a poet and offer his works – this sense of a writer completely in charge of her material is what makes Frances Oliver so pleasingly grown-up.

Glasgow Herald

**Girl in a Freudian Slip:**
'I hope your memoir gets the attention it deserves – it is so interesting and alive'

A S Byatt, (Possession, The Children's' Book etc., etc.)

www.ingramcontent.com/pod-product-compliance
Lightning Source LLC
Chambersburg PA
CBHW072228190626
46809CB00017B/1463